THE VENGEFUL VILLAIN AND THE CURSED TREASURE

A POINT MUSE COZY PARANORMAL MYSTERY
BOOK 6

KELLY ETHAN

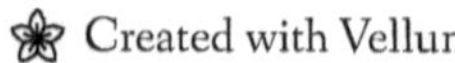 Created with Vellum

A shout out to all those that have helped me with this series.
You rock!!

THE VENGEFUL VILLAIN AND THE
CURSED TREASURE

A POINT MUSE COZY PARANORMAL
MYSTERY BOOK 6

**There's a murderous treasure hunt, a vengeful
villain hunting prey and a nosy Librarian
turned sleuth.
Let the mayhem begin.**

An all-expenses paid weekend away at a mysterious
treasure hunters' island paradise. At least that's how
Elspeth Harrow explained it to her granddaughter... She
lied.

Xandie Meyers, aka Librarian to the supernatural Great
Library of Alexandria, and her family of nosy, Harrow
witches, are back in the thick of a new murder investigation.
But this one involves a ghost, a vengeful villain, a cursed
treasure and a mouthy parrot screaming 'pieces of eight'.

Xandie has no choice but to swing into Sherlock Librarian
mode or walk the plank...

If you like snarky dialogue, murder and mayhem then you'll love the next installment in Kelly Ethan's Point Muse Cozy Paranormal Mystery series.

Unlock the mayhem of The Vengeful Villain and the Cursed Treasure!

lously high stiletto heels. Another man and Henry followed her. Xandie sighed and dropped Elspeth's bag on the ground.

"Excuse my family. All self-entitled, even my reclusive uncle." Another man, an identical carbon copy, without the plump middle section of his twin brother, sidled up to Xandie.

"It's fine. I'm here to help," Xandie replied through gritted teeth.

"You need me for anything, I'm happy to help. Herb's the name." He ran a finger down Xandie's arm. "Anything at all. Just call."

Ew. Xandie shook off the man's hand. "You can help with the bags right now."

Herb winced and pointed to his elbow. "Old tennis injury, I'm afraid. No lifting." He grimaced as he moved the arm.

The Hedgewater family did not impress Xandie at all. She glared at flirty Herb's retreating back. *"Tennis injury my..."*

"Probably drink related." David hauled up an old-fashioned luggage trolley and piled it to the top with matching bags. "He has a reputation as a lush, the playboy of the family. He recently lost his job as an online trader."

"I'm not surprised." Xandie dumped Elspeth's bag on the very top of the luggage trolley. "How do you know so much about the family?"

David shrugged. "The staff hears things. The old man who owns the house is sick, so the vultures have gathered."

"Money brings out the worst in people."

"They're in for a rude shock." David hauled the trolley up the path until it sat flat in front of the manor. "You should be able to get the bags inside now."

Xandie nodded her thanks and pushed the luggage trolley toward the entrance of the imposing Hedgewater Manor. A shiver tracked down her spine. The place gave her the heebies as her cousin Lila would say. Thankfully, Zach Braun, her police chief, bear shifter boyfriend, would join them in a few hours.

If a murder or two didn't delay him...

TWO

"What does she have in here? Rocks?" Xandie hefted the last of Gloria Hedgewater's bags onto the floor next to a fourposter. She ran a hand through gauzy curtains draped around the bed. Her finger snagged on a large hole. "This place looks luxurious on the surface but dig deeper and there are holes." *Literal ones.* Xandie wandered around the room, trailing her hand over the dusty chest of drawers. "And the housekeeper doesn't do dusting, obviously."

She scratched her neck as a prickly itch gnawed away at her skin. Xandie focused on the room, but nothing moved. No nasty, wealthy Hedgewater relatives critiquing her performance. Just a dusty, unloved room with somber paintings of unhappy looking subjects. Forcing the uncomfortable feeling away, Xandie dusted her hand off. "Last stop, Elspeth's pink bag." She stepped out into the hallway and softly closed the door behind her.

"Breaking and entering again, cousin?" Holly wandered up, crunching on birdseed, with a preening Petunia parrot on her shoulder.

"Seed bribery worked I take it."

Holly rubbed Petunia's head. "She's cute and very insightful."

"Petunia's a sweetheart. Find the will," Petunia squawked and settled back onto Holly's shoulder, looking pleased with herself.

"Find the will?" Xandie frowned. "Where on earth would the fluffy fiend have heard that?"

Holly shrugged without dislodging her sidekick. "Who knows? Parrots pick the weirdest things to mimic. Word is the guy's sick. Could it be his will she's talking about?"

His family members were already talking about the will? How tacky. Xandie hoisted Elspeth's bag. "Where's Elspeth's room?"

Holly pointed to the end of the portrait-decorated hallway. "Down to the end, hang a left, and it's the last door. She's in a suite."

Xandie groaned. "She gets a suite and we have a tiny attic room with three single beds at the top of the house?"

"Servants quarters, apparently. At least we don't have to share with Elspeth and Colin. Mom lost rock, paper, scissors." Holly nodded to Xandie and wandered back downstairs, mumbling to Petunia.

"The Harrows get crazier the longer I'm around them." Xandie trundled to the end of the hallway before turning and facing two decorative wooden doors with brass handles. She wrinkled her nose at all the odd portraits of frowning, disapproving Hedgewater relatives set on either side of the doors into the suite.

"Creepy. Glad the servants weren't important enough to warrant the personal touch of spooky Hedgewater ancestors in the attic room." All the staring eyes were off-putting, anyway.

Xandie kicked the door twice before Aunt Winifred

poked her head out. The exact opposite of both her sisters, Amelia and Miranda, Winifred had the same amber eyes but sported a blood-red dye job. Tiny at five feet two inches, she had a decidedly plump frame. Unlike animal empath and veterinarian, Amelia, or black ops, gun-toting Miranda, Winifred ran a potion and candle store in Point Muse.

"About time. Elspeth's ready to hex the entire household." Winifred reached out and dragged Xandie inside the spacious room.

"So not fair." She dumped the bag and took in the large wooden sleigh bed, a stone fireplace and sitting area, ornate wardrobes, and another small bedroom off the main room.

Elspeth sniffed as she came out of the adjacent bathroom. "About time. I guess you get the service you pay for."

"You aren't paying us."

"Exactly." Elspeth dropped onto the bed and sagged back before sitting upright with a wince. "At least we know whenever Harry wins a hand in poker, it ain't getting spent on the family mansion."

"I'm with you, doll face." Colin trotted out of the bathroom, his pug nose wrinkled. "The hot water is more like lukewarm, and the bed has heat-seeking springs."

"Colin." Xandie eyed the talking, flatulence-ridden pug. Elspeth had played Frankenstein with the poor dog to make him more attractive to the judges in a supernatural pet show. Or as her furious feline called him, pugenstein. The two animals had a hate/hate relationship. Both insulted each other nonstop and only ceased when Elspeth threatened bodily harm.

"Hey, you building those twigs up?" Colin pretended to flex his paws and shake his booty at Xandie.

"As long as you keep that wind machine away from me,

dog, you'll live." Xandie stared at Elspeth, unblinking, until her grandmother shifted uncomfortably.

"What? Why the death stare? I brought you with me for a weekend away. Where's the gratitude?"

"*As servants*. I had a fake blonde in stilettos order me to bring up her luggage. She packed enough to stay for a year. The caretaker had to find an old-fashioned luggage trolley so I could get it up to the house." Xandie stood, hands on hips.

"Hey, it was the only way to get you freeloaders in. Harry has always been a miser with money and jumped at the chance of free servants for the weekend." Elspeth checked out her rainbow-colored nails. "Besides, the rumor is he's sick and broke. Needs one more poker score." She scratched at a piece of wallpaper. "I think he needs cash to do some repairs before this cursed place falls apart."

"Cursed is right. Hedgewater Manor hasn't got the best reputation, and neither does Harry." Marjorie Penne, dragon, matriarch of the Pendrakon clan, and another poker crony of Elspeth's, swept into the room. Following close behind was Aggie Braun, bear shifter and mother to Xandie's boyfriend, Zach Braun.

"Marjorie." Xandie gave a quick squeeze to the dragon matriarch. With a smooth black and white streaked, chin-length bob and supercilious arched eyebrows, Marjorie projected the image of a grand dame. But in reality, the warm, caring woman with an acid tongue had become family. In other words, an Elspeth crony.

"My turn." Aggie wiggled around the dragon and snaffled Xandie into a tight hug. "Seems like months since I've seen you, girl. My Zachy needs to bring you around more often now that you've finally had that first date."

She and Zach had a few issues getting to their first date,

including a dead ex-girlfriend and a warrant for Zach's arrest for murder. Thankfully, they'd solved the murder and completed multiple dates since then. "You saw me last week, Aggie." Xandie tapped the bear shifter on the shoulder. "Can't breathe," she gasped.

"Whoops, don't know my strength. Sorry, honey." Aggie chortled and released Xandie to breathe.

Marjorie perused the room. Her top lip curled back, and a single fang appeared. "I think the rumor about Hedgewater's financial status is correct. The manor is a tad rundown."

Aggie snorted. "The entire family's rundown. I know Henry has cash from his real estate company and gives his brother a helping hand, but the rest of the family is too busy feuding over that silly treasure map to care about poor Harry's quality of life."

"The treasure map. I heard all about it from one of the online pirate groups I belong to. They swear the story's true." Winifred's eyes glowed at the thought of pirate treasure.

"The Hedgewater family, from Captain Horatio onward, have always been obsessed with finding the treasure. It's why so many of them have died."

Elspeth rolled her eyes. "Not a curse, but carelessness and avarice blinding them to the dangers of treasure hunting."

"Why so pious, grandmother? Isn't like you." Xandie eyed Elspeth suspiciously. When her grandmother acted innocent, everyone in the vicinity should run...

"Elspeth had a run-in or two with treasure hunters." Marjorie pointed a finger at her friend and grinned maliciously. "Someone swiped an entire Spanish galleon out from underneath her nose, or maybe it was the gold and emerald cross you wagered and lost to that gorgeous young treasure hunter?"

"Lies. All lies." Elspeth spat the words out. "That nefarious young man cheated and traded on his looks to distract me. Which, I might add, were glamored. He couldn't even be honest about that."

Xandie tutted. "Elspeth, the queen of chaos and mayhem, taken in by a good-looking confidence act. I'm ashamed to have you as our clan's matriarch." Xandie took one look at Elspeth's affronted face and couldn't help it. She burst out into deep belly laughs.

Winifred cleared her throat, but judging from the tears rolling down her cheeks, she agreed with her niece. Xandie took a deep breath to quell the laughter. Her grandmother was a grudge holder. She'd get even somehow with Xandie in a maximum humiliation fallout kind of way. But still worth it just to see her face.

"You'll keep, Librarian. Until you least expect it. Then I'll be there." Elspeth glared at her granddaughter.

Xandie twitched at the reminder of her day job. She'd cleared out all impending information requests and shelved the new stock. And she'd briefed her mother, Miranda, on Library operations. And Theo lurked nearby to lend a helping hand. But it still felt weird to be away from the Library and Point Muse. The Great Library of Alexandria had become a family member. The last few months had been non-stop issues, investigations, and the odd murder to sort out, but the sentient Library had become home. To leave it and the quirky supernatural-filled town of Point Muse behind had been more of a wrench than she'd expected.

"Sweetie, that sad puppy look slays me." Aggie smothered Xandie in kisses. "Zachy bear's delayed a little, but he'll be here soon. Don't worry."

Xandie had been worrying about the Library and not her bear shifter boyfriend, but she wasn't letting on to his romantic-at-heart mother. A police chief as backup in a spooky, decrepit, old house wasn't a bad thing. "I know. It's just this house gives me the creeps. Those paintings are all watching me."

Colin padded over to Xandie and rubbed against her jeans-clad leg. "I get you, kid. This place is freaky all right, and those eyes definitely move. I swear." Colin shuddered.

Xandie immediately leapt away from the animal. The last time he'd shuddered like that, a kidnapper had them tied up on a boat. Tuna and valerian sleeping drafts had not agreed with the pug's delicate constitution. Colin's radioactive wind was legendary in Point Muse. "Colin, don't you dare."

"Where's the love?" Colin pouted and shuffled back to Elspeth. "I swear, this place is more drafty than outside on those cliffs."

Elspeth picked up Colin and wrapped him in a blanket. "I'll get Harry to light the fire when we head downstairs for evening drinks. It'll be interesting to see what Lila whips up for us for dinner. Now scoot, I need time to prepare my magnificence before tonight."

Xandie hotfooted it out of Elspeth's suite, leaving the bear shifter and dragon to it. The last thing she needed was for Elspeth to ask her to draw a bath. Her grandmother would milk the lady of the manor part to the hilt, and Xandie didn't have the energy to deal with it.

Who knew what the wicked witch of Point Muse had planned for the weekend...

THREE

"Just helping out. *Blah. Blah. Blah.*" Xandie tugged on the way-too-short maid's uniform. She only stood at five foot five, but she'd paired the uniform with black leggings and heavy boots. Perfect for stomping on the unwanted attentions of an entitled Hedgewater.

Xandie kept her head down, muttering. She headed for the kitchen and Lila, so she totally missed the tiny woman coming out of a side door. She ran into the lady, and they both ended up spread-eagled on the worn floor. She flicked her frizzy, shoulder-length brown hair out of her face. "I am so sorry. Too busy fuming over the uniform to pay attention to my feet." Xandie gently pulled the tiny strawberry-blonde woman upright.

The woman blinked owlishly behind horn-rimmed glasses, awareness finally seeping in. "Oh, gosh. I didn't see you."

Xandie reached out and plucked a cobweb from the woman's tightly bound hair. A large smudge decorated her cheek. Strange, Xandie hadn't thought the manor so unloved that spiders had taken over? "I'm Xandie, the weekend help who apparently knocks down guests. I'm really sorry."

The woman giggled and stuck her hand out, gripping Xandie's with enthusiasm. "I'm not a guest. I'm Abigail Berry. I'm here to catalog and value Mr. Hedgewater's book collection."

"At least I didn't attack a guest, and since I'm not even being paid, they're lucky I turned up in this costume."

Abigail cleared her throat. "It *is* a tad short, but I like the leggings and the boots." She showed Xandie her jeans-clad legs with her own tiny pair of boots. "Much easier for climbing up and down ladders and looking at dusty books."

Xandie sighed. "I miss my own Library."

"You have a library?"

"I'm the Librarian to the Great Library of Alexandria, in Point Muse."

Sarah's eyes grew wide. "Wow. I heard that's an important job. I wonder if there's anything on the Hedgewaters?"

"If they're supernatural, the Library has it." And even if they weren't, the Library could normally do a work-around. Sentient libraries were crafty.

"The Hedgewaters are definitely supernatural. Starting with Captain Horatio, all the men in the family are weather mages, some stronger than others. The current crop of the family is all fairly weak. Plus, there's a ghost and a curse."

"Curse?" She'd deal with the ghost bit later.

Abigail nodded eagerly. "I've researched the Hedgewaters. The man who built the house is Captain Horatio, a.k.a. Harry Hedgewater. He came over from England as a fur trader but made most of his money as a privateer, a pirate. When the captain built the house, he brought his wife, Sarah, out." Abigail's face contorted for a moment before evening out. "She was a finder, a witch able to find anything, but kept isolated on the island. The captain was away on a trip when she supposedly got news he'd died. Brokenhearted, she threw herself off the cliff. He later turned up only to find out she'd killed herself. Her ghost supposedly still haunts the house."

"Really?" Xandie looked over her shoulder. This place looked exactly like the type of house a ghost would haunt.

Abigail smiled. "That's the story. At least *one* version. I think she had an affair and pirate Horatio killed her for it. The story is she cursed the treasure, so he'd never find it again. But most people prefer the other version."

"I'm all for a bit of intrigue." Xandie gestured to Abigail. "Again, I'm sorry about the demolition derby I subjected you to, but I need to get to the kitchen before more bloodshed happens."

"Nice to meet you, Xandie. I'm sure I'll see you at dinner."

Xandie rolled her eyes. "I'll be the one in the maid's outfit." She waved to Abigail and headed to the kitchen. Opening the door, Xandie instinctively ducked as a large metal serving spoon flew and slammed against the door.

"I. Am. Not. Impressed." Lila slapped at the puffy chef's hat on her head. "The housekeeper told me it's regulation for the chef to wear." Lila pointed at her white-jacketed chest. "I am not a chef. I'm a creator of culinary baked masterpieces. Not main courses. Dessert, I could swing, but main and appetizers?" Lila groaned and slumped on a stool lined up against a scarred wooden kitchen island.

"Take a breath, drama llama Lila." Xandie patted her cousin's stiff back. Each of the cousins had completely distinct personalities, but they melded together into a close-knit family that lived to squabble. Xandie, the bookaholic, enjoyed researching but jumped in feet first, always curious.

Lila, the dramatic one. Loud, expressive witchy baker with a sarcastic mouth. Holly, the youngest, *and* the quietest, liked to think plans through but was always available for backup and any verbal sparring with her cousins. In short, they were family. "One step at a time. Decide on your strongest dish, dessert first."

Lila perked up. "I already have blueberry lattice bars cooking." She sighed again. "But I've still got appetizers and main course to work out."

"Baking's your thing. What about mini smoked salmon and mushroom tarts? Point Muse loves those when you make them."

Lila clicked her fingers. "I've got the ingredients for that, and I can cheat a little. I spotted some pre-made tart shells in the pantry. But any main ideas, genius?"

Someone cleared their throat behind the girls. The housekeeper and the caretaker, David, stood in the kitchen's doorway.

He held up a small icebox. "A friend of mine dropped off some fresh salmon fillets yesterday. I figured you might want to use them tonight."

Lila leapt out of the chair, grabbed the icebox, and loaded it onto Xandie, before hugging the surprised caretaker.

"Thank you so much. We've been racking our brains trying to work out what to cook."

The housekeeper bit her lip and seemed to come to a decision. She extended her hand. "I should have been more welcoming to you three. Frankly, I'm overwhelmed. I'm Louisa Mathers, the housekeeper. Cooking is not my field of expertise, but I'll help you as much as I can."

Lila hugged the housekeeper tight. "You're a lifesaver."

Xandie pulled Lila's arms from around the stiffened

housekeeper. "Let the poor woman go. She's not your new toy. Besides, don't you have dinner to cook?"

"Right." Lila clapped her hands. "Xandie, you're the drinks lady, as is Holly. She's already headed out with a tray." She pointed to Louisa and David. "You two are my assistants. Now mush, people." She shoved a heavily laden tray at Xandie and pointed her toward the internal kitchen door.

Leaving her cousin to the now distant memory of her meltdown, Xandie navigated the wide hallway and entered the large games' room. Actually, a large room with a huge dining table and a stone fireplace. Threadbare velvet couches at one end and chairs and bookcases at the other. Currently, all the guests gathered together, including a frantic looking Holly in her own maid outfit but without the added protection of leggings.

"Where have you been? They drink like fishes. I can't get enough booze up to them."

"Why didn't you wear something under that outfit? The skirt's indecent."

Holly grimaced. "I didn't think of it?"

"The other little maid. I was hoping to see you." Herb Hedgewater stepped up next to Xandie, wavering a little on his feet, and placed his arm around her shoulders.

Xandie gritted her teeth and used her tray of drinks to create a wedge of space between them. "Would you like another drink? Water?"

Herbert shuddered. "Nary a drop of water shall pass my lips, sweet maiden."

"Never known you to be poetic, brother. Did you read a fortune cookie? Or some label on a wine bottle?" Another man, identical to Herb, slapped his brother's back, and caused his drink to slop over the slightly inebriated man's hand.

"Watch it, Harrison. This isn't a cheap drop, you know."

"Knowing the old skinflint, it probably is. Not that you would care. Any kind of buzz will do, the cheaper the better, hey, Herbert?" Harrison sneered at Xandie.

"Why you..." Xandie tilted her tray at the creep's rude face.

"Why, thank you, favorite granddaughter. I'd love a drink." Elspeth snatched a glass off the tray before they slid into Harrison's face. Elspeth turned to the inebriated Hedgewater and his insulting brother. "You wouldn't be rude to my favorite granddaughter, would you, gentlemen? Because that would be a very, very bad idea for your long-term health, boys."

"My nephews are idiots, but they don't have a death wish, Elspeth."

A tall spindly old man with the same ice-blue eyes glared at his nephews.

"No. I mean... Sorry. Too much to drink." Herb stumbled off and stopped in the corner of the room, followed by his nasty-mouthed brother, Harrison.

Petunia swept in and landed on the old man's shoulder. "Herbie is an idiot. Idiot," she squawked and looked pleased with herself.

"Quite right, Petunia dear." The old man ruffled the parrot's feathers.

"What's going on here, Hedgewater? You look like a walking corpse." Elspeth ran her gaze over the man. "Frankly, a corpse looks better than you do."

Harry Hedgewater croaked out a rusty-sounding laugh. "Life and bad choices have caught up with me, Elspeth. Cancer. I don't have long. That's why I called everyone here tonight. All the vultures gathering for one last hit at the money pot so to speak."

"Well, I never could resist one last time to beat you into a corner." Elspeth cackled, and the lights flickered . At the same instant, a gust of wind surged outside, causing the windows to rattle.

"Tone it down, Elspeth. This isn't Harrow House."

"Not my doing, girl. There's a storm brewing outside as well as inside."

A strange, short little man entered the room and whispered urgently into Hedgewater's ear. He nodded and waved the man off. "Seems our last guest has arrived."

A large-framed man, with bulky shoulders and a shiny bald head, strode into the room and slapped his leg. "The gang's all here." He sneered at the gathering.

"Clinton Reed," Aggie hissed, her grip tight on her wine glass. She lifted the glass and downed its contents in one large gulp.

"What's up, Aggie? Do you know him?" Holly sidled up to Aggie and offered her another drink.

"Reed's an ex-cop who worked with my husband, the Chief, for a while. As corrupt as they come. I always wondered if he took bribes from Hedgewater. Considering he's here, I guess I'm right."

"Why?" Xandie took stock of the room. Talk about a gathering of rogues, except for an odd few. Most of the room hated each other, had dodgy pasts, or nursed an ulterior motive for turning up. This weekend could get interesting.

"Hey, doll face, don't suppose you could get Baker Girl to hurry the food along? I'm wasting away here." Colin opened his pug eyes wide and stared plaintively at Xandie.

She placed the drinks tray on a nearby table and kneeled. "You only ate an hour ago."

"My big pugly body needs constant sustenance to maintain my magnificence," he whimpered.

Xandie sighed but stood. "A snack is all I'm getting you, okay?" Ignoring the whiny pug, Xandie headed for the kitchen. She paused at the door and listened for a moment. No sounds of swearing or wailing from Lila. Just a low murmuring noise. Xandie pushed the door open to a surprised David and Louisa huddled together and whispering intensely.

Louisa reared back, hand to chest. "You surprised me, Ms. Meyers."

"Sorry. After a small snack for a hungry pug. Where's Lila?"

David fiddled with a small radio until its reception cleared. "She had to grab something from her room. She'll be back down shortly."

Louisa bustled into the pantry and came out with a small container of cookies. "Petunia loves dry dog food, so we keep some on hand for her. Here." She extended the container to Xandie with a small smile.

Why such a strange atmosphere in the kitchen? If they were just talking, why so guilty? "Thanks." Xandie pointed to the radio. "Anything interesting?"

David grimaced. "That's what we were just talking about. The newscaster said there's a big storm on the way. Not surprising, I guess. It *is* storm season." He straightened and stared at the women. "I have to lock down the house and grounds. Make sure we're ready if we get a big blow." David nodded and disappeared outside.

Louisa sniffed and focused on Xandie. "As soon as your cousin's back downstairs, we'll serve dinner." She turned back to preparing plates.

And that was a dismissal. Xandie headed back to the

dining room and a starving Colin. No matter what those two said, that whole scene in the kitchen had been awkward. Something was definitely up at Hedgewater Manor, at least in the kitchen.

"About time, kid." Colin latched onto Xandie's leg as soon as she entered the room.

Xandie placed an open container on the floor but removed a handful of cookies. "Have at it, pug."

"My food. My food, nasty dog." Petunia swept in and tried to dive-bomb Colin's head.

Forestalling the epic battle, Xandie opened her hands. "I saved some for you, Petunia."

The bird stopped dive-bombing Colin and landed on Xandie's shoulder. "Librarian smart." The parrot delicately nibbled out of Xandie's open hand.

"Now that we're finally all here, I would like to announce why you're all gathered at the house." Harry nodded to the man carrying the briefcase. "This is Emmett South. He's my lawyer and has agreed to represent my interests, including my will and the deal I'm about to offer this room." He paused and waited for the murmurs to die down. "I'm dying. Cancer. *And* I'm broke. Bankrupt. I only have this island and the manor."

"What?" Henry yelled. "You've run through the entire inheritance? What about all your dodgy deals? All your profits?"

"Every single dollar," he confirmed. "That's why I have a deal for those brave or stupid enough to take it." Harry motioned the lawyer forward.

The man opened his briefcase, laid out a pile of contracts on the poker table, and stepped back.

Hedgewater continued, "Some of you are here for poker. To that end, I offer the only item of worth I still own.

My portion of the family treasure map. It will remain in my safe until the poker game tomorrow night. I offer you one game, high stakes. Winner takes the map. To the others not playing the game, I will offer you a set of clues. They correspond with the map. You will be free to hunt for the treasure at your leisure."

Abigail raised a timid hand. "Is the treasure, or the map, cursed?"

Hedgewater grated out a chuckle. "Yes, to both. The treasure has caused many a death in the family. And none of the males have ever been lucky in love or finances. The curse is real. That's why you'll sign a contract absolving me of any liability in case of death or injury."

"What do you get out of it, old man?" Elspeth considered Harry suspiciously.

"Twenty percent of whatever the successful treasure hunter finds. If I die before the hunters find the treasure, my percentage goes to my heir."

Henry Hedgewater, the twin brother, nodded meaningfully at his sons and daughter-in-law.

"My lawyer has placed the same set of clues in the envelopes next to the contracts. If you do not wish to play poker, you're welcome to take one." He raised his glass and smiled maliciously at the transfixed crowd. "The game's afoot, it seems."

FOUR

"A cursed treasure and he gets twenty percent before he dies?" Lila kicked a stone and huddled into her thick jacket. "I'll tell you who I'd curse and that's Elspeth for dragging me away from my bakery."

Holly clapped her hands and skipped around her grumpy cousin. "But treasure? Aren't you a little bit excited?"

"It's cursed. You'll find it and then die. That's how curses work."

Xandie agreed with her grumpy cousin. "I'm sure Elspeth can neutralize any bad woo-woo attached to the pirate booty. But do we want to buy into the treasure-hunting madness?"

"Tally-ho." Colin bolted past the women with a pirate hat hanging lopsided off his pug head.

"Bring on the gold rush." Elspeth danced into view, her waist-length, dead-straight, emerald green wig swaying wildly in the stiff breeze.

Lila jabbed a finger at her grandmother and her aunt

following closely behind. "I take it you're on board for the treasure hunt?"

"When I win that map, we'll combine it with your clues. We're shoo-ins to find it," Elspeth crowed.

"And the curse?"

"Bah humbug, curses. I'm the queen of hex. No paltry pirate curse can affect me." She looked encouragingly at her granddaughters. "Well? What's the clue?"

Xandie read the clue aloud. "The dark hole of my heart hides what you seek. Beware treacherous traps that lead the hunter astray. X marks the spot. My fortune found."

Lila frowned. "Why bother with the clues if you're sure you'll win the treasure map at the poker game?"

Elspeth waggled a finger at Lila. "Not just a pretty face, Baker Girl?"

"I'm pretty?" Lila threw Xandie a confused look. "Is she sick? She complimented me. Or was it sarcasm? Did she curse me?" Lila ran her hand over her face, searching for lumps and bumps mysteriously erupting.

"Calm down." Holly bit back laughter. "You're currently curse free."

Elspeth rolled her eyes. "Can we focus on treasure? Please?" Ignoring her family, she continued, "I know Harry. He's a pain in the behind and as dodgy as they come, but he ain't stupid. If the map alone could get him to the treasure, he'd be spending the gold already."

"You think the map combined with the clues is the key?"

Elspeth took a deep breath. "Nope." She exhaled, then cackled.

"Mother thinks the map isn't complete." Winifred lowered her voice. "Plenty of Hedgewaters have died looking for the treasure. She thinks a portion of the map detailing where the traps are hidden may have been removed."

"Thank you for stealing my show, daughter." Elspeth glared at Winifred.

Colin galloped up, his broad chest rising and falling at an erratic pace. "My girl doesn't like to share the limelight. She's a one-woman show."

"She's something all right," Lila whispered to Xandie.

Holly held out a hand. "How do we find the other piece?"

"Our Librarian is our ace in the hole. A pirate hole." Elspeth narrowed her eyes. "She's nosy, used to research, and without the added distraction of a body, should be able to find the missing piece of the map. Then boom...we're rich," Elspeth crowed and danced a jig on the spot.

Talk about pressure. "How did the map get damaged?"

"Now you can talk, Winifred. You like gossip, so crack on."

Winifred stepped closer to the girls. "Rumor has it, Captain Hedgewater's wife, Sarah, tore the map and hid her portion."

Lila frowned. "Wasn't she supposed to be so in love with her husband that when he disappeared, she threw herself off a cliff? Why ruin his map?"

"That's all I know. The Library might have more information."

"I spoke to Abigail yesterday. She's valuing and cataloging the contents of the Hedgewater Library. She mentioned another version of the story where Sarah had an affair and Hedgewater killed her. Maybe she stole the map on purpose so he couldn't find the treasure after she left him for her lover?" It wasn't such a stretch of Xandie's imagination to picture a woman in love with another man wanting to cause pain to the ex.

"Do what you do best and hit the Library. Look for the map or anything relating to the wife. Winifred, Colin, and I are heading back to the house. It's too windy out here for my baby. He might catch a cold," Elspeth cooed. "You three girls can search the grounds and then the house. Go over it with a fine-tooth comb. Now mush, treasure hunters." Elspeth clapped her hands to an accompanying boom of thunder.

Xandie eyed the gray sky. The wind had picked up, and the outlook was gloomy. A big storm was due to hit some time tonight. Hopefully, her boyfriend, Police Chief Zach Braun, would make it in time.

"If you're wondering, that wasn't Elspeth for once."

"Sorry?"

Holly pointed up. "The thunder is actually bad weather brewing. Not the wicked witch Elspeth Harrow."

Xandie shoved the clue into a pocket. "You heard our wicked matriarch. We need to search these grounds before the weather gets any worse."

Lila agreed. "Tell me we aren't splitting up. This place gives me the heebie-jeebies."

"I'm with you. This place is spooky. The paintings are always watching me." Holly grimaced.

Xandie hugged Holly. "No splitting up. Let's head to the boathouse and have a look around."

The three girls huddled together and walked as a group while the wind howled around them.

The stone boathouse loomed in front of them, white shutters slapping against the building. A dark figure, hammer in hand, appeared from the side of the boathouse.

Xandie screeched, high and tight. Her cousins joined her in a trio of girly shrieks.

"Geez. Calm down." David, the caretaker, flicked his hood off and glared at the women. "There's a storm coming, and I'm nailing all the shutters over the windows. What are you doing out here?"

What are we doing here? Xandie couldn't exactly tell him they were looking for clues to a treasure.

"Elspeth thinks she might've left something in the boathouse. Apparently, she poked around in here yesterday." Lila jumped in to save the day with the fib worthy of their wicked grandmother.

David paled. "Yeah, that old woman is scary. Have a look around but make it quick. I've got a lot of work to do today."

Nodding, Xandie slipped inside the boathouse, closing the door behind her cousins. David hadn't nailed the shutters over the windows yet, so weak light streamed into the boathouse. "Right, get searching. Yell if you find something that screams pirate treasure."

The girls split. Xandie headed for a bank of old cupboards and shelves. The boathouse was clean but crowded with junk. Old rowing boats, a small motorboat with its engine missing, safety gear, old oars, everything crowded in one small area. She ran her hand over the uneven wall. Nothing jumped out and screamed treasure to her. "Anything?"

Both Lila and Holly shook their heads. Xandie was about to give up on the search when her gaze caught on a pile of junk in the corner at the far end of the boathouse. A frown on her face, she marched across and stared at the mess of old tools, boxes of rubbish, coils of thick rope, and various bits and pieces of machinery from a time long gone. Then she realized something…something important.

The mess of rubbish wasn't leaning up against the rear wall as she'd assumed. It was all perfectly stacked and balanced to allow access to a small walkway between the garbage and the wall. *And* the two doors fitted into the wall.

She turned the old-fashioned knob on the first door and stepped into a bathroom, complete with a small handbasin. Old, yes, but by the look of the hand towel and cake of soap on the basin, perfectly clean and functional. She closed the door and tried the next one. It resisted all her efforts. Locked. No way to check it out. "What is so important that it had to be locked up?" she asked as Holly and Lila joined her.

Before the girls could answer her, Holly suddenly jumped as David nailed the first shutter closed over one of the windows. She gasped, then dragged in a deep breath. "Well, we're not going to get any answers right now. This has all been a bust. Let's get out of here and head to the summerhouse next. Before this storm overtakes us."

Xandie agreed, although her mind was still on the locked door. As the girls filed out, she paused in front of David. "Thanks, there's nothing inside, although we couldn't get into the locked room at the back."

"And Elspeth wouldn't have been able to either, so she couldn't have left anything in there," David replied. "That's *my* room which is why I keep it locked."

"I thought you'd be staying up at the main house?"

"I do have a room up there, off the kitchen, if I want it, but I prefer my own company most of the time." He gave a shudder. "Who wants to be at the beck and call of that crowd up there at the moment?"

"Very true. Unfortunately, because of Elspeth, we're it

for the moment. And speaking of Elspeth, we'd better get a move on. We'll leave you to it and try the summerhouse next."

The caretaker grunted. "Be quick, winds are getting worse."

Xandie nodded and joined her cousins on the path. "Let's get going."

Lila and Holly followed Xandie as they trudged across the grounds.

Almost a tiny cottage, the captain had constructed the summerhouse of the same red brick as the main house. Beautiful lead-light windows enclosed it, and a large ornate stone bench stood proudly in the front of the entrance. Xandie ran a hand over it. "This is lovely. Cold on my tush, but lovely." Xandie settled on the bench.

Wind howled past, and a clump of spruce trees nearby waved wildly.

Lila shivered. "You can sit, but I'm tearing the summerhouse apart. The faster we cross things off the list, the quicker we can hide inside the main house."

Holly agreed and followed Lila inside.

Sighing, Xandie sat straight up. Even with the looming storm and the dark clouds gathering, the summerhouse and the stone seat's outlook to the sea was breathtaking. Carved lettering on the bench's backrest caught Xandie's attention. She traced the letters. "The one who watched the sea." Captain Hedgewater had carved the bench for his supposedly lonely wife.

Maybe he'd left a clue on the seat somewhere. Xandie dropped to the ground and ran her hand under the bench. Something rough grabbed the skin on her fingertips. Xandie pulled out her phone and turned the light to shine underneath the bench. Rough carved initials, S.H. L–2, were gouged into the underside. She frowned. The writing looked nothing like the elegant script engraved on the back of the bench. Had someone else defaced the underside? *Is this the eighteen hundreds version of I was here?*

"Nothing." Holly slumped dejectedly on the stone bench. "Only garden tools, a potting bench, and some tables and chairs. Mostly covered in cobwebs."

Lila stood next to a still crouched Xandie. "Please, don't kneel to me. I don't need adoration. My baking gifts are available to all."

"Fool." Xandie angled her phone at the initials again. "What do you think?"

Holly and Lila crowded in, peering under the bench.

"*S.H.* Sarah Hedgewater?" Lila pursed her lips and thought. "What does *L–2* mean?"

Holly stood and dusted her jeans. "No clue, but we need to get to the graveyard before the rain starts."

Xandie eyed the now-black sky, intermittently highlighted by flashes of light. "Graveyard it is."

Lila nudged Holly. "You should feel right at home, Death Girl."

Holly rolled her eyes. "I'm ignoring you so we can get our soon-to-be-hit-by-lightning tushes inside."

The trio followed a weaving path to the other side of the small island. Covered with small, wooded areas and open pockets of landscaped gardens, Sarah Island was beautiful in an isolated and austere kind of way.

A high metal fence surrounded the Hedgewater cemetery, and large gates heralded the entrance. Xandie came to a screaming stop beside the gates. Wind howled like a vengeful ghost, and the air filled with the clanking of metal fences moving in the wind.

"Can we not go in and say we did?"

"Lightweight. You're our great sleuth? Doer of great idiotic deeds, deeds that normally put you and everyone else in danger. Now you're checking out?" Lila snuck up behind Xandie and shoved her through the open gates.

"Traitor." Xandie sighed and straightened. Elspeth had given them their orders, and it never paid to annoy the person who could put warts on your nose or hex your underwear drawer closed. "Spread out. See what you can find. At least this place is small."

Old gravestones dotted the landscape, some more unloved than others. Weeds mixed with flowers tangled around the stone headpieces. Small statues lined a path that led to the center of the graveyard where a plinth stood as a centerpiece. "I'll take the big one." Xandie pointed to the large stone and made a beeline toward it.

A mix of dark and light gray stone, the column soared above the rest of the graveyard. Ignoring the height, it was a relatively plain marker. Xandie read the words engraved on the stone. "Sarah, wife of Horatio." Xandie traced the words. Another smaller line caught Xandie's attention. "*An empty grave lies undisturbed. Taken by the sea too early.*" Interestingly, the marker had no death date recorded. The cool stone bit into the warmth of Xandie's hand.

"They put up a gravestone even though she fell off the cliff and they had no body to bury?" Lila joined her cousin.

"Well, if you listen to Abigail, she didn't throw herself off the cliff, her husband killed her. The stone proves her rumor. Lost to the sea definitely means no body."

"Hedgewater was a wife killer." Holly joined her cousins.

"If you believe Abigail's story. And everyone except Abigail thinks Sarah killed herself." Xandie ducked as the wind blew a small branch their way. A shriek sounded above their heads, a metallic grind of anger and passion. Xandie wiped her palms against her jeans. "I hope that was the metal fence moving in the wind and not the angry reply of a vengeful ghost."

Holly's eyes flickered silver for a moment before sliding back to the normal amber.

Lila gritted her teeth. "Since our resident banshee's eyes only go silver when someone's supposed to die, I vote we hightail it back to the house and relative safety."

Well, as safe as a house with a pack of rival treasure hunters could be...

FIVE

"Fetch this. Carry that. What am I, a servant?" Xandie grumbled as she stalked down the front stone stairs of Hedgewater Manor.

"Actually, doll face, I guess for this weekend, you actually are." Colin huffed and wiggled under Xandie's arm.

"So help me pug, if you go *before* I put you on the ground, I will smother you with the heaviest Library book I can find." Xandie carefully lowered the pug to the ground. "Get to it. The storm will be here soon." Xandie shivered and sheltered against the side of the manor house. At the moment, only a light drizzle of rain had touched the ground. But the wind roared over the island. The housekeeper, Louisa, had heard on the radio all ferry services were canceled. Which put paid to Braun visiting the island. "Come on, Colin."

He spun around and growled at Xandie. "It's hard to go with someone watching. I have performance anxiety issues."

Xandie ran her hands up and down her arms to warm

up. "Since when? Every time I see you, you're letting loose with something noxious."

"What can I say? I have a delicate constitution. But this place is different." Colin spared a glance over his shoulder toward the dark graveyard. "Ever get the feeling this place is waiting for something to happen?"

While Xandie privately agreed with the pug, she didn't want him to get a big head. "I know *I'm* waiting for something to happen."

Colin walked around in a circle, sniffing the ground, until he froze. Every hair stood on edge as a low growl emanated from his pug throat.

"Seriously, dog, your growl isn't scary. Give it up and just go."

"Open your eyes, Librarian. We've got company, and I don't think she's here for the poker night."

Xandie squinted in the graveyard's direction and like Colin, every hair on her body stood to attention. A wispy pulsing light in the shape of a woman's outline, with long floating tendrils of hair, hovered over the area. "Trick of the light?"

"It's dark. No lights out near the boneyard."

Xandie grasped at straws. "Weird lightning? Sea gases? Anything but the obvious?"

Colin whimpered as the light drifted a little closer. "Suddenly, I don't have any performance issues at all."

"Ew, Colin." Xandie couldn't blame him. She had a sudden urge to visit the bathroom and lock herself in.

The light gathered in motion and surged toward the house as the front door slammed open, Holly highlighted in the doorway.

"Holly? Head back inside. I think we have a ghost issue."

Colin bolted next to Xandie and leaned into her. "I don't think the banshee's listening right now."

Colin was right. Holly wasn't in control; the Harrow banshee was. She raised her head, staring sightless at the storm ahead. Her eyes were a wash of silver, no amber visible.

The wispy figure surged toward Holly, its high-pitched wail combining with the banshee's as she tilted her head back and screamed for death, the sound like the scrape of fingernails on a blackboard.

Xandie shuddered and collected Colin, racing toward Holly. Catching her cousin around the waist with her other arm, she dragged both her and the pug inside the manor and slammed the door behind her. Xandie dropped Colin to the floor and caught Holly as her cousin slumped against the closed door.

"Whoa, has Holly tippled out of Elspeth's hip flask?" Lila asked, joining her cousins in the hallway.

"Could you help me, please? She isn't as light as she looks."

Lila reached for Holly's other arm, and they hauled her upright. "What happened?"

"Banshee and ghost had a scream-off while Colin was on a potty trip."

The girls dragged Holly into the nearest room with Colin following behind.

"Man, freaky. Ghosts and banshees. What a wild ride. Wonder who the dead body will be?" Colin plonked down on a threadbare rug that graced the center of the hoarders' delight of a library.

Placing Holly on a dusty couch, Xandie took a slow turn around the room. Hedgewater's library was nothing like her own Library in Point Muse. Rickety shelves took up every available space, with the couch and a small table only just squeezed in. Dust covered all available surfaces like a thick snowdrift. Unlike Point Muse, this Library didn't gleam like a proud literary lady.

A noise at the entrance to the room had Xandie spinning toward the doorway. Abigail, the assessor employed to catalog the contents of the library, stood there, juggling a pile of books in her arms.

"What happened? Is she okay?" Abigail shoved the books onto the floor behind a sheet and bustled forward.

Lila shrugged. "Harrow mixed with banshee genes. It's a crapshoot. She'll be fine in a few moments."

Abigail paled. "Banshee? Does that mean someone's going to die since she screamed?"

"I guess that might depend on the ghost." Colin scratched his ear and wandered over to Abigail to rub against her bare legs.

"Ghost?" Abigail's eyes widened.

Xandie coughed and pointed at Colin who was peering up Abigail's skirt. "Um, you might want to move."

"Spoil my fun, sweet cheeks." Colin pouted but moved away and curled up on the threadbare rug in preparation for a nap.

Abigail grimaced and took another step away from the pug. She focused on Xandie. "You mentioned a ghost?"

"Turns out Sarah Hedgewater never left the island, even if the sea carried away her body."

Abigail clapped her hands. "The other version of the story's right, isn't it? Hedgewater the pirate killed her, and now her ghost wants the island."

"Seems like it." Xandie rubbed her forehead. She honestly just wanted a quiet weekend away. Of course, with the Harrow family, that'd probably never happen. "You told me about the other version of Sarah's death. What other information do you have on her?"

"Oh." Abigail smiled weakly. "I know a little. I have an interest in pirates."

"You and everyone else." Lila leaned over Holly as she fluttered her eyes. "I'm going to go get Elspeth. Holly has normally woken up by now after a vision. Xandie, keep an eye on her." Lila considered Abigail. "It would be helpful if you grabbed Holly a drink of water."

"I'm supposed to stay here and catalog." Abigail moved her hand around the crowded library.

"Five minutes won't hurt. Now scoot. We don't have long before the poker game starts." Lila grabbed Abigail's arm and tugged her out of the room.

Xandie crouched next to Holly and fanned her face with a hand. She needed a proper fan to make a difference. Glancing around the room, Xandie spotted a box full of old-fashioned clothing wedged between two ornately carved bookcases. "Might have a vintage fan I can use on Holly." Picking her way through the minefield of boxes, Xandie leaned against the bookcase as she rummaged. "Eureka." Xandie held up an ornate wooden fan with images of forget-me-not flowers painted on it. She used her free hand to push herself up. As she did, Xandie heard a weird click as the bookcase shifted under her hand.

She slid the fan into her pocket, stood, and pushed the bookcase a few inches to the right. A sliver of a dark shadowed passage appeared. "Hidden passageway." Xandie's inner Nancy Drew perked up. She gave the bookcase another push, and the sliver enlarged. The opening behind the bookcase seemed small but had a darkened passage off it. "Why have a secret passage in a library? And where does it lead?"

"Xandie?" Holly's weak voice trembled in the air.

Ghost-busting and investigating secret passages would have to wait. Xandie pulled the bookcase over the passage entrance, then made her way back to the couch and her cousin.

"Hey, cuz. How are you feeling?"

Holly pushed herself upright, rubbing her head. "I have a thumper of a headache."

"Might be because of the scream-off you had with the ghost of the murdered Sarah Hedgewater."

"Remind me not to do that ever again."

"Can't trust you all to investigate without one of you getting hurt, can I?" Elspeth tsked and flounced up next to Holly, her short, emerald green, nineteen-twenties style flapper wig swinging against her chin.

"Not my fault. I banshee shrieked, and some ghost got involved," Holly grumped and blew the bangs out of her eyes.

"Excuses. Here." Elspeth shoved a blue crystal bottle at Holly. "Take a swig. You'll be better soon."

Abigail popped out from behind Elspeth with her glass of water held out, observing the proceedings.

Holly eyed the potion suspiciously. "What's in it?"

"Hecate's sake, banshee. Woman up and swig." Lila snatched the bottle and shoved it in Holly's face.

Holly grabbed the bottle and chugged the liquid down, gagging. She reached for Abigail's glass of water and downed it in one gulp. "This is by far the most disgusting potion I've ever tasted."

"Everyone's a critic." Elspeth sniffed. "Now, banshee, tell us of your vision."

"All I know is that death's stalking Hedgewater Manor, and tonight's the night."

Abigail snickered, then covered her mouth with her hand. "Sorry, that's rude. Death and misfortune have always plagued the Hedgewaters."

"What do you mean?" Holly eyed Abigail questioningly.

"Since Sarah died, the family has had numerous unexplained deaths and bad luck. Food poisoning, bankruptcy, runaway wives, accidents. You name it, they've experienced it."

"Well." Holly stood and stretched. "I guess tonight won't be any different."

Elspeth rubbed her hands with glee. "I love it when a plan comes together. Plus, death adds a little spice to the night, don't you think?" Cackling, Elspeth stomped toward the entrance to the library. "Now. Scoot. We've a treasure map to win." Elspeth reached the door and spun to face her family. She threw something at her feet, and black smoke wreathed her figure until it covered her completely. "I said *scoot*," a deep voice boomed out, shaking the shelves and windows in the Library before the smoke dissipated to reveal nothing.

"She takes all that seriously, doesn't she?" Abigail shook her head, amazement showing on her face.

"You mean the wicked witch act?" Xandie rolled her eyes. "She's the original wicked witch, at least of Point Muse. We're sure she survives on the life energy of innocents."

"You get used to it." Lila stopped Holly with a hand on her arm. She waved Abigail on. "You go ahead. I just want to make sure my cousin's okay."

Nodding, Abigail slipped out of the room.

"You're concerned about me?" Holly fluttered her eyes at Lila. "That's so sweet."

Lila gagged. "I may vomit. What I want to know is our game plan for tonight. If we have a death in the cards, what do we do?"

"There's nothing we can do. Let Elspeth play her wicked poker game, and we have to make sure she doesn't end up in the morgue."

Colin took that moment to give up on his nap in the center of the library. He rose and trotted past the cousins. "Better get a boogie on, or the old girl will hex you."

He wasn't wrong, Elspeth held a serious grudge when her plans didn't go the way she wanted. Xandie hurried into the games' room. All the curtains were closed, and the fire flared bright in the stone hearth. An immense wooden table stood center stage with a darkened cloth over it. Large, ornate bookcases stood to attention on one wall, and a few old couches lined in threadbare velvet sat between two windows that faced the table.

"About time." Elspeth turned to face Harry Hedgewater and his tame lawyer. "We're all here. Let's get this cursed poker game on the road."

"Quite right, Elspeth." Harry glared at his brother. "Are you playing or not, Henry?"

Harry's twin brother stepped up to the table and laid a hand on one seat. "I'm a Hedgewater. That map should stay in the family."

"And that's why I'm playing, Daddy dearest." Herbert Hedgewater stood next to his father.

The power flickered overhead, plunging the room into darkness for a few seconds before surging back, bright as ever.

Abigail frowned. "I'll pop into the kitchen and speak to the housekeeper and caretaker. They might need to check on the generator." With a nod to the other guests in the room, she disappeared out the door.

"Everyone taking part, please stand by a chair." Harry gestured at the table.

Aggie, Elspeth, Marjorie, and Clinton Reed all stepped to a chair.

Harry moved to his own chair at the head of the table. "I won't be playing. Instead of that, I'll hold the prize."

The lawyer stepped forward and opened his silver briefcase, showing a yellowed, partially torn map to the room.

Harry sat, and the lawyer placed the open briefcase in front of him. "My lawyer, Emmett South, will act as the dealer. If everyone will sit, we'll begin.

Xandie cast a worried glance around the room. Aside from the poker players, only Xandie, her cousins, and Henry Hedgewater's eldest son and his wife watched.

Windows rattled as a nasty gust of wind and rain slammed against the house. Having Braun staying at the manor would have made her much happier. But with this weather, there was no chance of him arriving soon. Xandie wandered over to the French doors on one side of the room and tugged the drape open.

With the storm and fog and rain obscuring the landscape, there wasn't much to see. Unless a flash of lightning lit the outside up like daylight. She shivered as a whisper of fog drifted closer to the door. At least she hoped it was fog. The window flew open opposite the table and rain poured in. Lila and Holly rushed to secure the window as the elder Hedgewater twin and his wife huddled near the fire.

"It's the ghost. I know it is." Gloria pointed a bejeweled finger at her husband. "This night won't end well."

Xandie privately agreed with the brassy blonde as an

inexplicable gust of wind snuffed the fire out with a sizzle and a hiss.

Ignoring the commotion, the poker players focused on the cards dealt to them by the lawyer.

Harry held up the briefcase. "Remember, the stakes and my twenty percent."

The lights flickered again, flaring bright with a mighty gust of wind that shook the house. The chandelier above the poker table winked out, plunging the room into darkness.

Xandie gasped as wind roared past her. The French doors flew open again, and a bulky figure stood silhouetted in the doorway.

Shrieks echoed as the heavy games' room door leading out to the hallway flung open with the bang. A long undulating shriek of fury filled the room and a flickering wisp of mist hovered near the poker table. A guttural moan sounded, along with the crash of a chair falling. With no warning, the lights blazed on, illuminating the crumpled figure of Harry Hedgewater. Face down. Collapsed on the floor with an antique style stiletto sticking out of his back.

"He's dead. It's the ghost," Gloria shrieked from somewhere near the now unlit fireplace.

Clinton Reed bolted around the table and opened the briefcase that had fallen to the floor. "It's gone. The map's gone."

The figure illuminated in the door frame stepped forward and removed his raincoat. *"A murder and a robbery. Just another night at home with the Harrow family..."*

SIX

Xandie sagged in relief. "You definitely know how to make an entrance, Braun."

Zach Braun, chief of police and Xandie's boyfriend, gave her a glancing kiss on the cheek. "I need everything I've got to keep up with you Harrows." He dropped his raincoat on a chair and closed the French doors behind him. "Another murder?" He strode to the body and took a pulse. "Definitely dead. Everyone away from the table. Please don't touch anything."

The housekeeper, followed by David the caretaker and Abigail, rushed into the room. Louisa gasped as she spotted her employer's body.

David placed an arm around her shoulders and led the housekeeper to a seat.

"It's the ghost, isn't it?" Abigail moved shakily to the couch and dropped onto it.

"No such thing as a ghost," Elspeth hissed. "Just some murderous thief taking my treasure map."

Henry Hedgewater drew himself up. "That's a family

heirloom. Now that Harry has passed away, as his next closest relative, it belongs to me." He tapped his chest.

"That's nice and all, Hedgewater, but we signed contracts." Clinton Reed kicked the empty briefcase. "We all came here for a poker game. If we can find the map, I don't see why we can't run the game, anyway."

Braun stepped forward, hands in the air. "The first thing we need to do is secure Mr. Hedgewater's body. All of you will remain here while we search the house. Then you'll be escorted to your rooms where you'll remain until you're interviewed. More law enforcement support is already on the way and will be here tomorrow. Do I make myself clear?"

While everyone nodded, Clinton Reed stepped forward, his chin jutting out. "See here, Braun, I used to be on the job too. I can investigate as well as you can." Clinton balanced his large frame and flexed his arm muscles.

"Thanks for the offer, but this is still Point Muse jurisdiction, and I'm the police chief. I'm good with conducting the investigation myself." Braun pointed to Xandie and her cousins. "I've already deputized the Librarian and Lila and Holly Harrow until reinforcements arrive tomorrow. But you can definitely help with body removal."

Clinton scowled at Braun then stomped across to the far side of the room

Braun crossed to the housekeeper and caretaker and had a quick word before turning back to Xandie and her cousins.

"Seriously, deputies? That's a reach." Holly winked at the police chief.

"You make do with what you've got. At least you three have investigative experience, and I can trust you not to take a bribe."

"I don't know, Xandie's love of sweets is epic. She might be open for chocolate bribes." Lila chortled until Xandie dug an elbow into her ribs.

"We're happy to help, Zach." Her poor bear shifter looked exhausted. Xandie shuddered to think what the crossing from Point Muse must have been like with the storm cracking overhead.

Aggie slapped her son on the back. "Love seeing you put that double-dealing lowlife in his place. Your father hated that man."

"I take it Clinton Reed has a reputation?" Reed had an over-the-top character that made you like him or hate him. His physical appearance may have been intimidating once but had long gone from muscle to fat. Still, Xandie was happy to stay as far away from him as she could.

"Let's just say Clinton was always open to the highest bidder. Even as a cop. He and Harry Hedgewater had a deal. Clinton would hear of a treasure find through the police grapevine and let Hedgewater know about it. Then Harry would sweep in and snatch it up." Elspeth plucked out a hipflask and chugged a gulp down.

Xandie couldn't begrudge her grandmother her Witchshine. Elspeth, robbed of her savage game of poker, needed some kind of consolation. Hedgewater's death and the theft of the map had put paid to her planned poker victory.

Braun motioned to the caretaker as Louisa handed him a thick blanket. He spent a few minutes assessing the body before carefully wrapping it in the housekeeper's blanket. The caretaker helped him stand, and they carried the body out together.

"Poor Uncle Hedgewater," Gloria wailed from a seat next to the fireplace.

"Now, dear. The police will find the map and the killer." Harrison Hedgewater patted his wife's shoulder, careful not to disturb her hair.

Henry, the victim's twin brother, pointed at Emmett, the lawyer. "You still haven't answered me. Those contracts are void, right? Since I'm the closest living relative, the map and the island belong to me."

Emmett cleared his throat and patted down his stringy gray comb over. "The heir will inherit the island and the map, if it's found."

"See?" Henry yelled across to Clinton then smirked visibly at the red ex-policeman. "I'm the heir. Those contracts are void."

Emmett broke in. "As to that, until the will's read, and the heir confirmed, one should not assume."

Henry scoffed at the lawyer. "I'm his twin brother. Who else would inherit?"

"A month ago, Mr. Hedgewater made changes to his will."

"What?" The entire clan exploded into loud denials.

A whoosh of wind overhead and a peculiar rattling noise made Xandie duck automatically.

"Petunia free. Can't lock Petunia away. Save the pirate. Save." Petunia cackled maniacally and swept down to perch on Colin's back.

Colin, apparently over his issues with the parrot, clucked in sympathy. "Poor girl. You're too late. The old pirate bought the farm."

Petunia sagged against Colin, her feathers drooping.

"Poor little birdie." Winifred knelt next to Colin and carefully stroked the bird's feathers. "Do you miss your master?"

"Petunia late. Can't keep Petunia locked up." The bird waggled her head against Winifred's fingers.

"I'll keep an eye on Petunia. She listens to me." Louisa extended an arm and whistled.

Petunia lifted into the air, landing delicately on Louisa's arm. She rubbed her head on Louisa, cooing.

Something about Petunia's words niggled at Xandie's sleuthing bones. "She said Petunia free. Can't keep Petunia locked up."

Lila raised an eyebrow at her cousin. "And?"

Holly snapped her fingers. "Someone locked the bird up, but why?"

"Petunia said save the master. Maybe she heard something about his death and wanted to warn him?"

"That bird is an avian menace but smart." Marjorie Penne, matriarch of the Pendrakon clan, sauntered up to the group. "Someone wanted to stop the flighty animal from divulging her secrets, so they locked her up. Would have to be someone she trusted. Otherwise, they'd never get close to her."

Xandie nodded. "Good point, Marjorie."

"I'm full of good ideas."

"You're certainly full of something, Penne." Elspeth snickered, then offered Aggie and Marjorie her hipflask.

The three women hunched over the flask, whispering and cackling.

Xandie shuddered. "They remind me of the three hags from Macbeth, cackling and plotting wicked deeds." She scanned the room. Definite groups had formed. The Hedgewaters huddled near the fireplace, whispering fiercely. Reed now stood next to the lawyer, gesturing wildly, while the poor lawyer tried to ignore him. Louisa and Petunia stood near Winifred and Colin. Abigail sat by herself on the couch near the end windows, facing the poker table. The three cackling cronies were near the center of the room, and Xandie and her cousins were off to the side.

The room seemed undisturbed except for the empty briefcase, overturned chair, and a puddle of blood... and a very old ivory fan the body must've hidden. Xandie placed a hand on her jeans pocket on the fan she'd scavenged in the Library. The old box of clothing and accessories had other fans... Maybe that included the one on the bloody floor. But what did a fan have to do with killing Harry Hedgewater?

"Penny for your thoughts?" Braun stepped up next to Xandie. "What are you thinking, Sherlock Librarian?"

"Someone wanted Harry dead." Xandie walked over to the spot where Harry died and knelt. She fished out the fan from her pocket and considered both. They looked similar, painted flowers and ornate handles. But there was one big difference. The fan hidden under the body had a long, thin, hollow cavity in the handle.

"I take it you found something?" Braun kneeled next to Xandie, his arm pressed against hers.

"I think the knife in Harry's back may have been hidden in the fan." Xandie pointed to the blood-covered fan on the floor.

"Looks old." Braun reached into his pocket and drew out an evidence bag.

"You came prepared for murder?"

Braun winked at Xandie. "I came prepared for anything a Harrow could dish out."

Xandie fought the rising tide of heat that threatened to engulf her pale cheeks. "I think the fan may have come from the library. There's a whole box of old clothing and fans. I saw it when Holly had an episode earlier."

"The knife in Hedgewater's back was a stiletto. It could

have fitted in the hollow perfectly. Who had access to the library?"

Xandie grimaced. "Pretty much everyone in the house. Abigail cataloged and valued the books, but anyone's allowed in. Plus, I found a passage behind a bookcase. Which means anyone might clandestinely have entered without a person noticing."

"Figures." Braun straightened and helped Xandie to stand. "The body's isolated in the cool room. It should be safe enough until my brothers get here tomorrow."

"How did you get through to them? Phone lines are down and there's no reception."

Braun snorted. "Because it's a storm and all the Harrows are together on an isolated island, I figured a body might turn up. Before I left Point Muse, I told Caleb and Riley to head out here first thing tomorrow."

"Forward thinking, Chief Braun." Xandie winked at her bear shifter boyfriend. He'd gone from being a cantankerous pain in her patootie to actively supporting and encouraging her sleuthing ways.

"I aim to please." He shared a warm smile with Xandie before sighing and reverting to cop mode. "It's late. We need to get everyone up to their rooms and take witness statements."

Xandie grimaced. "There's one other thing to think of, though."

"What's that?"

"Dinner never did get served. How long before someone, probably Gloria, starts moaning and groaning that they didn't get fed?" She gave a deep sigh, knowing what she was about to suggest would mean more work for her and her cousins. "How about if we put some of the appetizers and a pot of coffee on a tray and take it to each room as we go in to interview them? Then they can't complain."

"Wanna bet?" Braun said with a shake of his head. "But it's a good idea. I'll give you a hand with the trays. *Then* we'll call it a night."

Call it a night? Xandie would be happy to call off the entire weekend. Lesson to be learned here...

Never trust Elspeth when she offers you a weekend away.

SEVEN

"You ain't takin' me alive, copper."

"Braun doesn't get paid enough for this." Xandie knocked again on the housekeeper's door. "It's Xandie Meyers. I'm supposed to take your witness statement."

The door creaked open and Petunia swept over and trailed her claws through Xandie's hair.

"No pieces of eight for you," Petunia squawked again, flapping her wings wildly at Xandie's face.

"Come here, you silly fusspot." Louisa offered Petunia a couple of seeds and coaxed her back onto her perch.

"I don't think she likes me." Balancing the tray on one hand, Xandie ran her other hand through her hair, making sure Petunia hadn't left any bird deposits behind.

"She doesn't like anyone much, but there's always been a bird at the manor since Captain Hedgewater built it. It's tradition." Louisa shrugged. "She isn't so bad and is a natural mimic. It can be quite entertaining."

Xandie entered the room and placed the tray on the bedside table. Then she dropped down onto the lone chair in the room. "We delivered trays to everyone so no one

54

could complain they didn't get fed. Thought you might like one too."

"Thank you, my dear."

Xandie watched her lift one of the appetizers from the tray, then said, "Earlier tonight, Petunia said no one could lock her up, and she wanted to save Hedgewater. Who would lock Petunia up?"

Instead of looking amused at Xandie's words, Louisa appeared considering.

"Petunia's allowed free reign of the house. She can roam wherever she wants. She's quite well house-trained. At bedtime, she has a cage that lives in the kitchen normally. Nice and warm."

"So, why would she talk about someone locking her up?"

Louisa tapped her cheek, thinking. "I don't know, but she's a mimic. If she heard someone threatening Harry, her first inclination would be to warn him. She's very bright." Louisa smoothed the feathers around Petunia's head.

The no-nonsense housekeeper seemed to have a warm side. Xandie jiggled her notepad. "Can you tell me what you saw tonight?"

Back to business, Louisa straightened. "Absolutely nothing until after everyone else discovered the murder. I was in the kitchen, following Lila's orders on the appetizers."

"Did you see anything around the house that stood out as different? Did any of the guests act out of character?"

The housekeeper let out a bark of laughter just as another gust of wind and rain rattled the windows.

Petunia shivered on her perch and tucked her head into her feathers.

"Something funny?"

"Everyone's treasure mad. Obsessed with that damn

map. Hedgewater's family are all gold hungry. Look at how his brother, Henry, badgered poor Emmett about the will. Hard to spot a murderer in that lot."

The lawyer who changed Harry Hedgewater's will not so long ago. "Emmett's been here recently?"

"He's kept on retainer, so he pops up regularly. He earns his pay, since some of Harry's schemes aren't quite as legal as most people think."

Not as much of a surprise to people as Louisa thought it might be. "Same with Clinton Reed? I heard he would notify Mr. Hedgewater when anything treasure-related came up."

Louisa sniffed, her disdain obvious. "That Mr. Reed. As corrupt as they come. Probably why he and Harry got along so well. Both devious sharks that would turn on you at the first hint of weakness."

Wow, hate much? "If you disliked your employer so much, why stay?" For the first time since Xandie had entered the room, the housekeeper looked flustered.

"I'm a single mother and I need a job. You do what you have to."

Child? "I didn't realize. Is your child living with his father?"

Louisa pursed her lips like she'd sucked on a lemon. "His father has never been in the picture. My son's an adult now. He makes his own decisions."

And now Louisa looked unimpressed. *Interesting...* "You heard and saw nothing other than the greedy antics of the treasure hunters?"

"David and I were in the kitchen, readying the appetizers. Lights flickered off and on, and then that book valuer, Abigail, came running in talking about the generator. The caretaker had a quick look, and we all checked on the electricity in the games' room. That's when we saw the body."

All three alibied each other. The rest of the guests, including the Harrows and their cronies, were in the games' room. Who could have killed Hedgewater? "Thank you, Louisa. I appreciate your honesty. I suggest you lock yourself in your room for the rest of the night."

"Doesn't really help much. Supposedly, there are passages throughout the whole house. But at least I have my early warning system." The housekeeper patted Petunia on the now snoring head. "Besides, I'd be more worried about Harry's twin brother, Henry. If someone's after the treasure, taking out the next in line to inherit would be my next move. Then again..." Louisa shrugged. "I'm just the housekeeper. What do I know about family legacy, treasure maps, and cursed treasure?"

Bitter much? "Thanks again." Xandie waved to Petunia and quickly slipped into the hallway. She waited until she heard a click of the lock behind her.

Something about Louisa rubbed Xandie's sleuthing instincts the wrong way. The woman was definitely hiding something. But was it murder? "Riddled with passages? Looks like I'll get no sleep tonight." Xandie checked her list for her last witness statement. Abigail, the book valuer. At least she didn't have to interview that playboy lech, Herbert Hedgewater. Lila had drawn that short straw.

Xandie collected another tray from the kitchen and, clutching her notepad under one arm, strode down the hallway to Abigail's room. Unlike the three cousins stuck in the attic, Abigail had scored a room in the guest wing. Not too far away from Elspeth's suite. There was one thing about sleeping in the attic. She didn't have to walk past all those horrible Hedgewater portraits constantly. A shiver trailed down Xandie's spine, and she fought the urge to scratch the back of her neck. She scooted past a small painting and then jerked to a halt before reversing to stare at the portrait.

Something about this portrait drew her in, almost as if the woman painted wanted her to stop. In fact, the portrait seemed so real that if this was Scooby Doo, the eyes would have moved. Xandie scanned the painting. The subject was a woman in her early twenties, her auburn hair twisted on top of her head in a pile of massive ringlets. She wore a dress with a high square neck, and the sleeves were narrow and flowed out at her wrist. The ornate dress seemed narrow at the waist but bunched up the back before flowing behind her. The dress was a rich brown with a turquoise over dress with white and gold stitching. The woman must've been well off.

She stood staring out at Xandie with sad hazel eyes, a hand extended as if to stop her. A round table with a small gold-edged open journal with a feather quill resting across it featured in the corner of the painting. Xandie noticed that, behind the woman, partially obstructed by the small table, was a golden birdcage, and fluttering at the edge of the painting was a parrot that looked suspiciously like Petunia. She peered closer at an engraved plaque that lined up with the bottom edge of the frame. "Sarah and Petunia, eighteen seventy-eight."

Sarah Hedgewater and her parrot, Petunia. Unless the current Hedgewater parrot was a ghost, then modern day Petunia must be a descendant of Sarah Hedgewater's original parrot.

"Poor woman." The whole impression of the painting was sadness and loneliness. Goes to show you, a person might have wealth, but money didn't make you happy. "No wonder you haunt this place. I'd hate the manor too."

A loud crash echoed from above her head. Xandie left off her art appreciation to trudge to her last interview. Knowing her luck, Colin had probably let loose a radioactive flatulence bomb in the attic room and the house was loudly and slowly collapsing in on itself. She paused at Abigail's door and rapped softly. "Abigail? It's Xandie. I've brought you some supper, and I have to take your witness statement."

A series of bumps sounded loudly from the room. But the door eventually opened, and Abigail gestured Xandie inside. "Am I your last stop? You look exhausted."

"I'm okay." It wasn't Xandie who looked tired, but Abigail. In fact, her cheeks were bright red, and her strawberry-blonde hair stuck up in wispy tufts on one side. Hopefully, the woman wasn't getting sick. The last thing this house needed after a murder was a bout of flu.

"I'm afraid I can't help much. I was in the kitchen when the murder happened." Abigail moved a pile of books off the chair onto the floor so Xandie could put the tray down. "Sorry about the mess. I have a tendency to bring my work home."

Xandie could relate, but Abigail was definitely a packrat. Books covered every available surface. Abigail's room was actually worse than the library downstairs. The only empty space was a small bookcase that sat against the far wall.

"Anything you can remember would be really helpful."

"Okay." Abigail settled herself against her bed's headboard. "I was with everyone in Sarah's sitting room."

Xandie broke in. "Sitting room? I thought it was the games' room?"

"Originally, Sarah claimed it as a reading and sitting room. The library was the captain's domain, not that he'd read a book in his life. All the books in the current library were apparently Sarah's. When she died, Hedgewater turned it into his games' room. Probably just to spite her." Abigail sniffed.

If most of the books in the library were hers, there was a good bet the clothing, fans, and hidden stiletto might be as well. Xandie needed to search the library properly. Sarah may have left a diary or some papers or even her supposed piece of the map. She continued with her interrogation. "Keep going, Abigail."

"The power flickered off and on, so I asked David, the caretaker, if the generator was working properly. I found Louisa and him in the kitchen, whispering together."

"What were they talking about? Could you hear?"

"Not much. A few words. *It's not time yet, be patient. We'll get what we're owed.* That type of thing." Abigail frowned. "They looked pretty close, if you know what I mean. I felt awkward interrupting them."

So, Louisa and David knew each other more than the housekeeper and the caretaker relationship. What were they owed?

Abigail continued, "I told them about the power issues, and David went down to the basement to check on the generator. Didn't take long before he came back. Said it was fine. I headed back. Then the power went out. Louisa and David found me outside Sarah's room, and we entered together. That's when we saw Mr. Hedgewater." Abigail closed her eyes for a moment and swallowed heavily. "Not a sight I'm likely to forget."

"Upsetting for everyone."

"Yes, but the way Louisa reacted, and even David,

seemed over the top. Don't get me wrong, it's horrible. But I'm more worried about who's going to pay me. But that's just my opinion."

"Thanks, Abigail. I appreciate you talking to me."

Xandie stood but paused for a moment. "I saw Sarah's painting out in the hall. She looks so lonely."

Abigail sighed. "I know. I stare at that painting every time I walk past. Must've been a hard life being a pirate's wife."

"She had Petunia. Our Petunia's ancestor?"

"Apparently the original Petunia came out with Sarah from England, and there's always been a winged descendant at the house."

"Did Sarah have a journal or diary?" It might have clues to the whereabouts of a portion of the map."

Abigail shook her head. "Not that I've found yet. The library might look like a hoarder's paradise, but I've gone through most of the books. I haven't found a diary of hers." Abigail cast a perfunctory smile at Xandie.

Interesting... Abigail said no diary, but the painting definitely featured an open journal with a quill pen. *Sounds like a diary to me.* Maybe Abigail hadn't found it yet? "Thanks for your honesty. Lock your door and get some sleep. Hopefully, the storm will blow itself out by tomorrow."

"I will." Abigail opened the door. "Try to get some sleep yourself, Xandie. Everything will look better in the morning."

Xandie nodded and headed back to the kitchen. A quick clean up and then she could go to bed. She groaned when she saw there was one tray still sitting on the bench. So, who hadn't received their supper?

She ran through the list of guests and staff in her mind,

ticking them off on her fingers. "Damn it. We forgot David. I wonder if anyone thought to interview him?"

Braun wasn't around so, with a sigh, she realized she'd have to do it. Raiding the pantry, she found a flask and quickly filled it with hot coffee. Then she wrapped some of the appetizers in baking paper and foil and slid them into a shopping bag hanging on the back of the kitchen door. Hanging on the same door was a heavy coat. Xandie dragged it down and slipped it on, pulling the hood up to cover her head before grabbing the flask and shopping bag and letting herself out of the kitchen.

She ran around the side of the house until she connected with the path that ran down to the boathouse. She could see slivers of light through the shutters over the windows facing her, so David was still up. She belted on the shutters and then carried on to the door of the boatshed and thumped on it with a clenched fist. It took a few moments and then she heard the locks click and the door opened. Not waiting for an invitation, she pushed her way inside and dragged the hood of the coat down.

"What the heck are you doing out in this?" he demanded.

She struggled to catch her breath and then said, "I brought you some supper seeing we all missed dinner." She held out the shopping bag and the flask of coffee.

He took them from her and grabbed her arm, sighing as he guided her toward his room. "In this weather? Stupid." He shook his head. "You'd better come in for a moment, then I'll walk you back."

The room was more like a bedroom/sitting room with a single bed on one end and two lounge chairs at the other end, with a small kitchenette on one side. No stove but a microwave. Xandie grimaced. "Sorry, I didn't know you could cook something for yourself. I just didn't want you to go hungry."

He set the coffee flask and the shopping bag down on the small kitchen bench and turned over one of the framed photos standing on top of the microwave before Xandie got more than a glimpse of David and an older woman standing with their arms across each other's shoulders. Xandie frowned at the gesture.

"I'm used to doing for myself, but I thank you for thinking of me." He pointed to one of the chairs. "Do you want to sit down?"

"No, I won't. I'm dripping." She grinned and ran a hand down the wet coat. "It's raining out there, you know."

He gave what sounded suspiciously like a chuckle. "Ah, yeah, I did know, and I need to get you back before this storm gets any worse."

He grabbed a coat off a hook on the side wall, but before he could shrug it on, she wanted to ask him a few questions. "David, is there anything you can add to what happened this evening? Anything you saw or suspected?"

He shook his head. "No, by the time I got to the games' room, it was a done deal. Hedgewater had already been killed. As to who did it... Who knows, but I think any of those greedy treasure hunters would be capable of it. They don't care a damn for anything but money. So much for family, eh?"

He slipped into his coat and gestured to the door of his room. "Let's get you back to the main house."

Knowing she wasn't going to get any more out of him, she let him guide her outside and rush her back to the kitchen door. Once back inside, she shed the borrowed coat and headed to the back stairs that led up to the attic and her shared room. Hopefully, Braun and the others had more luck finding a suspect than she had. So far, Louisa and David were the only slightly shady options she had. She grabbed the door handle to her room and gave the handle a sharp twist, but the door refused to open. Xandie thumped on the wood. "Hey, why lock the door?"

"It's not us. Give it a push. Put your Librarian muscle into it," Lila hollered through the wooden door.

Xandie put her shoulder to the door and used her weight to fling it open. She stumbled into the room. "What happened?" Clothing lay strewn on the floor, sheets ripped off the beds, a small desk and chair turned over. And Lila and Holly stood in the middle of the mess with disgruntled expressions. "Don't tell me. One of you upset Elspeth, and she hit our room with a tornado hex?"

"No. We found it like this. We finished our interviews and headed up here a few minutes ago."

"I heard a thump earlier from above, but I just thought Colin had exploded or was raiding us for illicit food."

"Colin's with Elspeth and Winifred. They're moving furniture around for barricades, and Elspeth's hexing up an intruder alert."

Xandie kicked a pile of clothing. Whoever had ransacked the room was after something. Something Xandie had no clue about. For once in her sleuthing career, she had no idea who the prime suspect was.

She had a horrible feeling the body count would rise before they got off this cursed island...

EIGHT

"Hecate's toenails. I curse the rocks in this mattress." Xandie groaned as she rolled to her side. She lifted her head and peered around the attic room. Holly and Lila had disappeared, probably woken earlier and headed downstairs to organize breakfast.

Xandie pushed herself to her feet and stretched the kinks out of her spine. They'd been up late last night, righting their ransacked room. Plus being in the attic, the storm had sounded like a freight train overhead. Not to mention the crashing of shutters against the house. Xandie drew open the curtains and peered outside through the tiny window. Trees and branches littered the ground, and pools of water and mud covered the once immaculate grounds. The wind still blew, and the gray skies hadn't cleared yet. Hopefully, the storm wouldn't turn back and hit them a second time.

Xandie shivered as an icy breeze touched the back of her neck. Which was strange, as most of last night, the attic had been toasty warm. No draft at all. She tracked the cool breeze to a portion of the room that had an old-fashioned, plain mirror attached to the wood paneling of the wall. The mirror was less than two feet wide and dirty as heck. Xandie ran a hand over the surface. Part of the mirror had bubbled, and little waves rippled over the glass. Even the frame had uneven corners and patchy coloring.

It looked old, but as old as Sarah Hedgewater? Xandie ran her hand around the edges. "No draft." She moved to the wood paneling, repeated the same motion with her hand, and an icy chill from the side of the paneling buffeted her hand. "No reason a wall panel should have a draft coming around it unless something lay behind." Pressing on the panel, Xandie was rewarded by a click. It swung open. "Louisa was right. Passages *are* everywhere."

Thankfully, she hadn't bothered to change last night in case of a late-night murder victim. The only thing Xandie needed was a flashlight. She rummaged through Holly's bag and came up with an old-fashioned metal flashlight. She wrote a quick note telling her cousins what she was doing and stuck it to the mirror. Next, she propped the passage door open...*just in case.* "Right. Indiana Meyers, let's go exploring." Xandie switched her light on and flashed it around inside the passage.

A landing with a set of stairs heading down greeted her. Xandie tested the floor, but the boards seemed strong enough. She stepped in and directed the flashlight down the stairs. "Looks sturdy." As long as she avoided any spiders or cobwebs, Xandie was fine. She tested each step as she crept her way down the stairwell. She flicked her light over the red brick walls. Cobwebs and spiders galore overhead, but from her height down, thankfully bare of eight-legged critters.

Xandie moved farther into the passage and faced a dead end. "No fair." She ran a hand over the wall, searching for any pressure plate that would trigger another open door. Toward the far side of the dead end, the brick became wood paneling again. A small portion of the panel shifted under her hand. "Eureka."

A hidden door swung inward this time. She carefully poked her head out into the hallway where the guest bedrooms were. Stepping out, Xandie brushed herself down in case of cobwebs. Surprisingly enough, she was critter free, which made her wonder if that passageway had been clean for a reason. Like a late night ransack of her room? Carefully closing the wood panel, Xandie stared up at the mysterious Sarah's portrait. "Hiding so many secrets must get terrifying, hey, Sarah?"

"Does lack of suspects mean you start talking to yourself?" Braun leaned against the wall next to Sarah Hedgewater's portrait and winked.

"I have Harrow blood; the crazy is strong enough." Xandie tried to hide the flashlight behind her back.

Braun reached behind Xandie's back and drew the flashlight out. "Is there anything you want to tell me, Meyers?"

Xandie coughed. "Someone *may* have searched our room last night, and I *may* have found a hidden passage from the attic room to the hallway on this level."

"Hypothetically, of course. Because you definitely would have told me if your room was searched. Wouldn't you, Xandie?" Braun arched a sardonic eyebrow.

"Maybe not so hypothetical." Xandie pointed to the panel. "There's a door right next to you."

"I'm not interested in a hidden door, more in what you have to say."

"Okay, I may have snooped and found the passage. Nothing happened, wasn't in danger. All good."

"Did you find anything in the interviews or the secret passage?"

"Just the passage and nothing interesting in the interviews, except for the fact Abigail thinks Louisa and David are way too close for housekeeper and caretaker. You?"

"Everyone hates each other and thinks they deserve the map and the treasure, even if it's cursed." Braun toyed with a lock of Xandie's frizzy brown hair.

"Treasure hunting. It's a disease." Xandie rolled her eyes. "The hex queen is sure she can remove any curse the treasure may have. Plus, we found another version of the Sarah Hedgewater story. She had an affair, stole a portion of the Hedgewater map, and her husband killed her, and that's where the curse came from."

"Wouldn't surprise me. The Hedgewaters have always obsessed over money and their inability to keep it." Braun straightened off the wall. "Caleb and Riley will be here any minute. But we're not allowing anyone off the island just yet."

"Since the killer has to be one of us, that's probably smart," Xandie supplied.

"Exactly." Braun leaned down and brushed Xandie on the nose with a brief kiss. "At least we can spend time together. Even if it's in the middle of another murder investigation."

"Chief? Excuse me, Chief Braun? I have a complaint to make." Gloria Hedgewater stormed up, her brassy blonde hair flapping indignantly.

"Yes, Mrs. Hedgewater?"

"You and your appointed deputies." Gloria shot Xandie a disdainful glare. "They've left our room in a horrible mess. Looks like a tornado. I demand your deputies right the mess they caused." She stood, hands on hips.

Xandie and Braun exchanged a glance. "Neither myself nor my deputies have searched any rooms. Is there anything missing?"

Gloria's annoyed facade crumbled, and her hand went up to her mouth. "I didn't check. I thought it was the deputies throwing their weight around."

"Nope. None of the deputies are that petty."

Bursting into tears, Gloria sagged against Braun. "Someone hates us enough to tear our room apart."

Xandie gave in to her boyfriend's pleading glance and gently detached the devastated woman.

Gloria swung around and stared at Xandie, tears forgotten. "My diamonds," she screeched and took off at a stiletto-wobbling pace.

Xandie trailed behind her.

"My room being searched wasn't a one-off?"

"Obviously not. I expect everyone's rooms have been searched." Braun scratched his cheek. "Any idea what the culprit was after?"

"Maybe the treasure map, but then that means the killer and the thief are two different people. Because if the killer had the map, why bother searching everyone's rooms?"

Gloria popped out of her room. "The door was open when I came back up. I checked and my diamond bracelet's missing. It took Harrison years to buy me one," she wailed.

"Chief?" Caleb and Riley Braun, twins and younger brothers to Zach, stood frowning behind them.

Braun blew out a relieved breath. "Right. Caleb, you take Mrs. Hedgewater's statement about her stolen jewelry. Riley, you're with me. We need to check each of the guest rooms. Xandie..." Zach trailed off.

"Yes, boss?"

"You do whatever you need to. Just don't get yourself killed."

"Harrow genes, can't promise anything." Xandie winked and carried on down the hallway to Elspeth's suite. She rapped on the door and then walked in. "Oh, Hecate's bleeding eyes. I'm blind." She covered her eyes with one hand and tried to make it to the bed without collapsing.

"No discrimination, please. Dogs have feelings too." Colin flicked his rainbow-colored wig over his shoulder as he continued to prance around, his neon pink ballerina tutu flapping as he moved.

"I think it looks marvelous," Winifred gushed as she blew the pug a kiss.

Xandie lowered her fingers, steeling herself for the color explosion that was Colin. "I take it everyone's bored?"

Winifred shrugged. "You know what Mother's like. Keep her occupied or..."

"Or she ends up in jail for causing chaos and mayhem."

"That's my doll face. She's a keeper." Colin pranced up to Xandie. "Don't suppose you brought snacks? I've danced up a powerful hunger, and my girl hasn't come back yet."

"What?" Xandie jerked. "Elspeth isn't here?"

"She went looking for nibbles for me. My blood sugar gets low when I don't eat." Colin stared righteously at Xandie.

"There's nothing wrong with your blood sugar that a good diet wouldn't fix."

"Winifred covered Colin's ears. "Don't say the *D word*, you'll upset him. We'll never get the smell out of this room."

"There's a murderer haunting this house and Elspeth's out on her own?"

Winifred bent over, body shaking as heaves of laughter

bellowed out. "I'd be more worried about the killer. This is Elspeth we're talking about."

Good point. Her grandmother probably *was* the most lethal person on the island and that included the killer.

"You're right, but we still need to be careful. I'll head down and keep an eye on her. Braun's brothers have arrived, so at least he has back-up."

Colin trotted behind Xandie as she moved to the door. "Remind doll face about my snacks, kid. I could waste away in the time she's taking to come back."

Xandie ignored Colin.

"Kid? Do you hear me?" Colin moaned, then trotted out into the hallway after Xandie. "Xandie girl? Snacks? Remember?" Groaning, he followed behind Xandie. "A pug's just gotta deal with his own snacks sometimes." Colin raised his voice at Xandie's retreating back. "I'm gonna go find my Elspeth myself. It's your fault if she blames you for starving me."

His plaintive wail followed her. "That dog has food issues."

"Aunt Amelia would say Elspeth is the one with the issues and Colin's just the recipient." Holly popped up next to Xandie, scaring the daylights out of her cousin.

Xandie put a hand over her racing heart. "We need a good bell on you."

"It's this place. Gives everyone the heebie-jeebies." Holly leaned forward, excitement spreading as a red flush across her pale cheeks. "There are so many passages in this house. It's like a Scooby Doo movie."

"I'm Velma. Brains before beauty...*or snacks.*" But her cousin wasn't far wrong. Xandie had found two passages so far. Who knows how many there were in the house? "How many passages?"

Holly nodded vigorously and pointed to a smudge of dirt on her nose. "I found one from the kitchen to the summerhouse, and I think Lila may have found a few."

"Speaking of our drama llama, where is Lila?"

"Right behind you, with a big problem."

When isn't there a problem when Harrows are involved?

NINE

"Don't tell me. Elspeth has caused some kind of hex-related drama?"

A frazzled Lila stood behind Xandie holding a tray full of breakfast food.

"No." Lila nodded at her full tray. "The lawyer asked for a tray in his room for breakfast this morning. He has to do the will reading today and wanted extra time to make sure everything was right."

"Makes sense," Holly murmured.

"But when I knock, there's no answer."

"Maybe he went downstairs for breakfast instead?"

"I don't think so, Xandie. He said he absolutely wasn't eating breakfast with those greedy jackals that are after him. He told me he wasn't letting anyone in except for me and his breakfast, and he was locking the door to keep all the treasure hunters out. Except when I delivered his breakfast, I didn't get an answer. So, I put my head in..."

"And?" Xandie and Holly chorused the word together.

"His chairs are turned over and there's blood on the floor."

"That's definitely trouble." Xandie grabbed the tray and handed it off to Holly. "Could you take this to the kitchen and then find Braun? Tell him we have a missing lawyer problem. *Discreetly*."

Holly saluted and grabbed the tray.

"Holly?" Xandie called out to her cousin. "See if you can track Elspeth down."

"I should get danger pay, or any pay for that matter, for dealing with my grandmother." Holly continued around the corner.

"She isn't wrong," Lila agreed.

Xandie gripped Lila's arms and turned her around. "Missing lawyer, remember?"

"Right." Lila followed Holly around the corner for a few meters before pulling up short at a door slightly ajar. She frowned. "That's strange."

"What's wrong?"

"I closed the door behind me. I didn't want anyone else seeing the room before we investigated."

Someone had snuck inside. Xandie put a finger to her lips and peered through the crack of the open door. Every few seconds, someone passed by. Someone definitely *not* the spindly lawyer. Xandie flung the door open and stepped in, hands on hips. "Anything I can help you with?"

Harrison Hedgewater jerked and spun around to face Xandie. "Excuse me? You've burst into a private room."

Seriously, this Hedgewater was cuckoo if he thought he could bluff her. "I burst in because we have a report of a missing lawyer. What's your excuse?"

"*Well... I...*" Harrison stuttered for a moment before carrying on. "He didn't join us for breakfast. Emmett's an old family friend, as you know. I thought I'd check on him." Harrison crossed his arms and stared righteously at Xandie.

"*Aha.*" Hedgewater was as bad at lying as the Harrows were.

"After finding the lawyer missing, you searched his room for something. Maybe the will?"

"Purely out of concern." Harrison seemed to dare Xandie to comment.

"All right then. I'm sure you're needed downstairs. Don't let me keep you." Xandie held the door wide open until the nosy Hedgewater left. She shut it quietly behind him. "What's the bet the will, more than the missing lawyer, drew him to the room?"

Lila leaned against the door. "Harrows don't take sucker bets. From the conversation I heard earlier between him and his wife, he needs the money as much as his playboy twin brother does."

"I thought good old Harrison and his dad Henry were flush and playboy wastrel, Herbert, was the bankrupt one?"

"Nope." Lila shook her head. "The entire clan can't hold on to cash. I'm betting old Henry's as desperate for the map as the rest of his family so he can snaffle the treasure. Then all those money worries are over, but it looks like ole Harrison doesn't trust daddy to share the wealth. That's why he searched the lawyer's room."

"Speaking of the lawyer." Xandie scanned the room. Lila was right, a struggle had definitely taken place. The chair near the desk was on its side. Xandie knelt next to the chair and slid it out of the way. Half a dozen small droplets of blood dotted the surrounding floor. Maybe someone had hit the lawyer to get him out of the way so they could search for the will? "Any sign of the will?"

Lila nudged the lawyer's briefcase, wedged partially under the bed, over to Xandie.

Xandie rifled through the contents. "Paperwork for

transferring the house to the next heir, contracts for the poker game, and..." Xandie lifted out a folded invoice. "Looks like Hedgewater gave the lawyer his marching orders." Xandie held out the invoice for Lila to read.

"Why do you say marching orders? Hedgewater could have just paid Emmett for his previous work."

Xandie pointed to a couple of sentences penned in a messy scrawl at the bottom of the page. "Golden handshake, old boy. You knew this day would come. A man can't serve two masters. Consider this your severance pay."

"Serve two masters?" Lila scrunched her nose. "The guy's a lawyer, so he must have multiple clients."

Xandie tapped her cheek thoughtfully. "The other clients wouldn't have mattered. But if he had a client who directly opposed Hedgewater's interests or had an interest himself that opposed Hedgewater's? That may have forced Harry to fire the lawyer after this weekend."

Lila took the invoice and scanned it. "That's interesting."

"What?" Xandie peered over her cousin's shoulder.

"The invoice." Lila read aloud, "Services paid in full for major addendum to the will and testament of Harry Hedgewater."

Xandie nibbled her lip. "Harry made a big change to his will recently. Maybe the rest of the Hedgewater clan had a reason to worry. What's the date of the will change? Does it say?"

"Couple of months ago, I think."

"I wonder if any of the Hedgewater clan have visited Sarah Island recently? Maybe one of them convinced our victim to change his will? That's why Harry died and the lawyer's missing."

"A Hedgewater is our killer?"

"Maybe." Xandie snorted. "But I've been known to be wrong before. Let's find Braun and let him know what's going on."

Lila handed the briefcase off to Xandie. "Plus, we still need to look for clues about the treasure or the map."

"Library's the best place for that."

Lila followed Xandie out of the lawyer's room, and they headed downstairs. "Do you believe in ghosts, Xandie?"

"Before this cursed weekend, my practical Librarian brain would have scoffed at you. But now..." Xandie shuddered. "I know what I saw when Holly went banshee. Sarah Hedgewater definitely haunts the manor."

"Can a ghost kill someone?"

"How should I know?" Xandie rolled her eyes. "You speak to Elspeth for that. Are you having an ectomorphic crisis?"

"Say what?"

"I've been watching too many b-grade movies," Xandie muttered. "Why do you ask, Lila?"

"First, this old house gives me the creeps. But when that poor man died, Holly and I were standing in a different area than you. We were on the other side of the room, near the bookcases. I swear when the lights went out, a cool breeze touched me." Lila rubbed the bare skin on her neck. "I said nothing because...I thought..." Lila ground to a halt.

"You thought we'd paint you with the Elspeth crazy brush?"

"Pretty much."

Xandie patted her cousin on the cheek. "We've all got Harrow genes, cousin. Crazy's bred into us. Sorry to burst your bubble, but what you felt was most likely another passage being used. Just means we have to search the games' room for a passage."

Holly popped her head through the open games' room door. "Get in line. Gold fever has hit Hedgewater Manor. Braun tried to lay down the law but isn't having much luck getting everyone to listen."

Xandie girded her mental loins. Judging by the multiple raised voices, her poor boyfriend wasn't having much luck getting anyone to listen. She stepped into the room.

"You have no right to stop us." Henry Hedgewater jutted his chin.

"I have every right since Sarah Island is in Point Muse law enforcement jurisdiction," Braun calmly returned verbal fire.

"This is Hedgewater land. Hedgewater treasure," Gloria screeched to the room.

"Ignore them. I have a contract." Clinton Reed flapped a piece of paper in the air.

Interestingly enough, it seemed like the corrupt ex-cop had finagled his own contract away from Emmett. Before or after someone had kidnapped the poor lawyer? "You found your contract, Mr. Reed? I thought the lawyer collected them all up after poor Mr. Hedgewater died." With a smile on her face, Xandie stepped up next to Zach, purposely keeping the lawyer's briefcase behind her back.

"He did. When I spoke to him this morning and raised my concerns, he gave me my signed contract back." The ex-cop dropped his hand and slapped the contract against his leg.

"Really?" Xandie let her voice trail off, letting doubt at Reed's story creep in. "When did you speak to him again?"

"Not that it's any of your business, Librarian, but I spoke to him this morning before breakfast." Reed puffed out his chest. "He listened to sense and gave me my contract."

Either Clinton spoke to the kidnapper through the door and that person had slid the contract underneath the door or Clinton had stolen the contract from the missing lawyer's discarded briefcase. Or the kidnapper *was* Reed. But which scenario was the right one? "Did you speak to the lawyer face-to-face, or just barge in and search the room when you realized he was missing?" *Go for the jugular, Xandie.*

"What are you accusing me of?"

Braun shot Xandie a questioning glance. "Answer my deputy's question."

The ex-cop sneered at Braun. "All you bear shifters are clannish. Sticking together."

Aggie stepped up next to Clinton and bared her teeth. "Answer the Librarian. You know what a temper we shifters have. Four bear shifters and one dragon in the room. Who knows what kind of damage could occur before we all calmed down?"

Marjorie snorted, a trickle of smoke drifting out of a nostril as she picked her teeth with a shining silver claw.

Clinton gritted his teeth. "Meddling bears. Fine. The door was open and the lawyer gone. His briefcase was on the floor, so I took back my contract. Happy?"

"You didn't think it might be a good idea to let me know the lawyer was missing?" Braun growled at the ex-cop.

Reed shoved his contract into a pants pocket. "What's the Braun family ever done for me? You'd find out, eventually."

"You mean Hedgewater didn't pay you. Why bother doing something that might end up as work?" Aggie muttered under a breath.

Xandie stepped into the fray. "The lawyer and his copy of the will are currently missing. We need to find him and then deal with the second problem."

Marjorie stopped snorting smoke. "What second problem, Alexandra?"

"Elspeth and Colin are missing." Xandie had an ominous feeling another body was in the cards.

Hopefully not my grandmother's...

TEN

Braun directed his reluctant troops. "We'll take the house room by room. Then head outside and comb the grounds. Each searcher has to have a partner for safety." Braun quickly split the house occupants up, putting any suspicious house guest with a police officer.

Xandie eyed Henry. Braun could have at least partnered her with someone she liked. She promised herself payback later. All she had to do was steal the man's secret honey stash. Her boyfriend would be putty in her hands. A maniacal, evil laugh echoed through Xandie's mind.

"Ms. Meyers? Are you okay? You have the strangest expression on your face." Henry Hedgewater peered worriedly at the Librarian.

"Just mentally plotting someone's downfall." Xandie dredged up a smile. "Braun assigned us the housekeeper and caretaker's quarters. Do you know their whereabouts?" She knew where they were, but she wanted to see just how knowledgeable this Henry Hedgewater was about the comings and goings in the house.

"Of course." Henry sniffed and then strode off toward

the kitchen. "Servants' quarters have always been at the side of the house or near the kitchen. Oh, and the attic, of course."

"Do you know about any passages in Hedgewater Manor?"

Henry scoffed. "A pirate built the original house. So, yes, it's covered in passages." He stopped at the entrance of the kitchen. "There's a passageway that leads to the basement and various other serving passages between rooms. That allowed servants to move around the house without being seen in the main residential area."

"Makes sense. Back in those days, servants weren't seen until needed."

"Correct. And of course, there's the cloakroom passage that leads to Harry's games' room."

Where he died. A coincidence? *Probably not.* "And the housekeeper's room?"

Sighing, Henry turned and headed down a smaller, less portrait-filled hallway. "Technically, Ms. Mathers should be housed in this room." Hedgewater pointed to a small room on the right.

Xandie poked her head in...*literally*. Since the room was so tiny, she'd be hard-pressed to fit anything else. "Snug."

"Quite. Instead, my brother installed her in what would have been historically the butler's quarters. Apparently, she needed more room."

This time, her searching partner opened a door on the left. Five times the size of the first room, still small compared to Elspeth's suite, but definitely livable.

"I'm sure you're experienced with rifling through people's lives. I'll wait outside while you dig through the trash." Henry grimaced and waved Xandie inside.

What a snob. "That's fine, Mr. Hedgewater. Please

don't leave the area though. It's for your safety." Xandie ignored his affirmative grunt and continued into Louisa's room. A single bed and desk, a thick rug on the floor, a pretty cut-glass lamp on the bedside table and a brass bird-cage with the door open. That was it. Nothing else in the room. And no different than it was when she'd visited Louisa the night before.

"Thief, thief. Cut your finger off." Petunia the parrot swept over Xandie's head, claws tangling in her hair.

"Hey, bird, get off. I wasn't stealing anything."

Petunia landed on the top of her cage. "Petunia's pretties hidden. Long time. Pretties all Petunia's."

Xandie held out a hand. "Calm down, Petunia. I promise I won't take your pretties. Would you show me how nice they are?"

The bird cocked her head to the side and considered Xandie. "Petunia like Library. Trust Library Girl, find truth." She hopped into her cage and clawed at something metal before dropping an object on the housekeeper's bed. Then she flew to the cage and came back with more items. She continued until a pile of pretty sparkling objects spread over the bed.

"Thanks, Petunia. Library Girl trusts you too." Xandie rifled through the pile and fished out Gloria's diamond bracelet. "Good taste, Petunia."

"Shiny. Petunia likes pretties."

Picking through the pile, Xandie separated a brass key with a small outline of a house engraved onto it. A key to somewhere might come in handy. "Petunia? Could I have the key for a little while? I promise to give it back."

Petunia bobbed her head. "Trust Library Girl. Solve the mystery. Release us."

Okay... "Thanks, Petunia." Xandie turned her attention

back to the pile of Petunia's pretties. A circular, rough metal piece scraped at the skin on her fingers as she trailed them through the pile. Xandie plucked it out.

"Pieces of eight. Paid in blood," Petunia squawked again and flew around the room, agitated.

"Calm down, bird." Petunia had been right. This was an old coin, probably copper. As Xandie scrubbed one side, an image of a lion holding a shield with a date of eighteen seventy at the base became clear.

"Treasure," Petunia squawked again.

Xandie stared at the coin. "Pirate booty?"

Petunia cackled and circled Xandie. "Trust the Library, solve the mystery." The bird hovered for a moment and then zoomed out the open door, obviously startling a still waiting Henry, since his curses reached Xandie's ears.

Pocketing the coin, Xandie piled the rest of the pretties, excluding Gloria's bracelet, back into the cage. "Thanks, Petunia." The parrot had somehow been near the treasure, if her cackles of treasure and the pirate coin was anything to go by.

"Are you done yet? We do have other things to do."

"Almost." Shoving the pirate booty to the back of her mind, Xandie searched the room methodically. She even lifted the mattress, but nothing seemed out of place. She opened the drawer of the small bedside table, empty except for a leather-bound book. Xandie read, "*History of the Maine Coastline.* Dry reading. But whatever floats her boat."

Xandie flicked through the pages until an old yellow photo fell out of a much younger Louisa, holding a little strawberry-blond boy with ice-blue eyes. Something familiar about the photo niggled at her. She'd have to work it out later. Since the sighs of Hedgewater's patience wearing out had reached epic levels, Xandie slid the photo back in the book and closed the drawer. She joined Hedgewater back in the hall.

"Did you find anything?"

"Nothing much except Gloria's stolen bracelet. I think Petunia's attracted to expensive, shiny objects." Xandie handed the bracelet to Gloria's father-in-law.

Henry chortled. "Shiny maybe, but this is mostly paste. Our family has had nothing expensive in our hands since Sarah Hedgewater cursed us."

"She didn't throw herself off the cliff because her love was missing at sea?"

"Not as such. From what the family understands, their marriage wasn't a happy one. Captain Hedgewater was away most of the time, and her attention wandered. He found out and there was a struggle. She hit him with a rock before falling to her death. He lost consciousness for a while. When he came to, he had a portion of the treasure map but no memory of Sarah taking the other half, how she died, or where he'd hidden the treasure." Hedgewater barked a laugh, this one more miserable than the first. "Since then, the family's mission is finding the treasure. Unfortunately, most of us have found financial ruin or death instead. Sometimes both."

"That's why you want the map. Because you need the money."

"Most of my finances are tied up with my brother's. We're almost bankrupt. My son's financial status isn't much better than my own."

"That's why Harrison was looking for the will."

Henry nodded. "That damn lawyer started seeing my brother weekly, a few months ago. Around the time the caretaker started working here. We thought Harry may have changed his will. That's why Harrison searched the lawyer's room."

"Your brother had the poem and the map. Why couldn't he find the treasure?"

"Most of the clan knew where the treasures were located, but we couldn't get to them. The portion of the map Sarah stole records the whereabouts of all the booby-traps Hedgewater laid. Other family members have tried to breach the treasure without the booby-trap coordinates and never made it out."

That's why Sarah's portion was so important. "Have you searched for her piece of the map?"

"For the map, her journal, anything we could find of hers. But we've seen nothing. No hint of anything that might help us find the treasure."

A journal? Abigail had said there wasn't one. "Hedgewater's wife had a journal?"

"Supposedly hidden somewhere in the house with clues to where her portion of the map is."

Xandie followed Henry out of the servants' section into the entrance area near the front door. To the side of the entrance was a small room. Xandie pointed to the cloakroom. "Is that where the passage is to the games' room?"

"Correct. Originally Sarah's sitting room, but it was turned into a games' room after she died. The passageway lets out near the bookcases at the end of the room."

"Thanks." Xandie fumbled in her pocket for the key she'd found in Petunia's purloined goodies. Taking a punt, she showed it to Henry. "Any idea what lock this key fits?"

Henry pointed to the house shape engraved on the handle. "That's the summerhouse. The key disappeared over fifty years ago."

Why would Petunia have a key to the summerhouse?

"I suggest we move forward in our search. We need to find the lawyer and that will." Henry strode toward the front door.

Xandie followed behind the soon-to-be Hedgewater heir. Henry had been surprisingly forthcoming. *Why?* "Not to be suspicious or anything, but why answer my questions so readily?"

Henry flung the front door open but paused and faced Xandie. "Because, unlike the rest of my family, I'm not stupid. If anyone finds the treasure without dying, it will be you. I'm hoping your moral, ethical, Librarian self will decide to gift the treasure back to the Hedgewater family." Henry bared his teeth in a parody of a smile and stomped outside, nearly bowling over Abigail.

"Whoops." Abigail sidestepped Henry. "Sorry. Didn't see you there, Mr. Hedgewater."

"Obviously." Henry headed outside toward the boathouse.

"I have a feeling that manners aren't an important quality for the Hedgewaters." Xandie stood next to Abigail on the front step of the house. "How did your searching go?"

"Louisa and I finished searching our assigned areas. I thought I'd head back to the manor library and keep cataloging. Even if Harry is dead, whoever takes the island over might still want the library valued. I hope so, anyway."

"It must take forever to go through each book, especially in that hoarders' delight."

"It takes time to deliver a quality value. My grandfather always told me a thorough job is a job well done."

"Is your grandfather in the book valuing business too?"

"He was. Been a family business for a very long time. He passed away four months ago." The smile dropped away from Abigail's face. "We received the Hedgewater job just before he died. He made me promise to continue his life's mission."

"And did you?"

"Well, here I am." Abigail spread her arms wide and stared up at the house, an unreadable expression on her face.

Xandie scanned the area for Henry, but he'd disappeared. "I need to get back to my search area. Do you know if anyone's checked the summerhouse?"

"That's Reed and Herbert's search area, but I saw sleazy Hedgewater near the boathouse, having a smoke break."

Was it a coincidence that Henry had headed that way? Had the eldest surviving Hedgewater hatched a plan to meet his wastrel of a son instead of searching? "Thanks, Abigail."

Xandie waved to Abigail and headed for the summerhouse, avoiding the various branches that lay scattered over the grounds. The immaculate English country garden landscaping had received a battering. Poor David had his work cut out for him reshaping the storm-ravaged garden.

She stopped near the summerhouse. The stone structure had escaped damage from the storm, although branches and small trees lay nearby. An especially large one had fallen just in front of the door. Xandie grunted as she tried to tug the branch out of the way.

"Need some help?" David dragged the tree off to the side.

"Thanks. I'm not sure if Reed and Herbert checked the summerhouse yet, but I thought I'd give it a quick once-over." Xandie tried the handle, but someone had locked it. She banged on the wooden door. "Hello? Is anyone there?"

A dog's raucous barking sounded, followed by, "Get us out of here, toots. I'm ready to blow."

That confirmed Colin's presence. Hopefully Elspeth and the lawyer were with him.

David yanked on the handle, then tried using his shoulder to shove the door open. "It's locked. He could never find the key, so Henry kept it open all the time."

Aha, Petunia's key. "I can help with that." Xandie extracted her engraved key and inserted it in the lock. At first, the key refused to turn, but after jiggling it a few times, Xandie turned the key and the door swung open. "Elspeth?" Xandie ran in and dropped to the ground next to her groaning grandmother as Colin ran past her. "What happened?"

David hurried up to the lawyer and worked on the ropes securing him.

"Some treasure-mad scallywag hit me on the head when I took my morning walk. I heard Colin rushing up behind me and then nothing. I woke to find both of us in here."

Xandie followed David's example and made quick work of the knots.

David supported the elderly man as he helped the lawyer to stand.

Visibly shaky, Emmett South leaned on David's arm. "I was preparing for bed last night and felt a draft on the back of my neck. The next thing I know, I'm in the summerhouse tied up. I tried yelling, but with the storm overhead, I had no chance of being heard. Then someone in a hooded coat dropped off an unconscious Elspeth and that stinky dog this morning." Emmett wrinkled his nose at Colin as he returned from outside.

"Hey, a pug's gotta do what a pug's gotta do. You're

lucky dinner wasn't tuna. It could have been much, much worse."

Xandie shuddered at the countless memories she had of Colin's horrifying stench. His sensitive stomach had come in handy upon occasion, but not when locked in a poorly ventilated summerhouse in the middle of a storm.

"Did you get a look at who the culprit was?" David tightened his grip on Emmett as he asked the question.

Wincing, Emmett shook his head. "No, it was dark, and they wore a bulky hooded coat. But they took the will and…" Emmett trailed off, blushing bright red.

What did the lawyer have to look so guilty about? Xandie clicked her fingers as the pirate penny dropped. "You stole the treasure map."

Emmett sighed and nodded. "I'm ashamed to admit I did. Greed got the better of me, I'm afraid. As Harry once said, a man cannot serve two masters. Obviously, someone worked out I had it and took steps to retrieve the map."

"Or someone went for the will and the map was a bonus," Elspeth joined in.

Everyone stared at the elderly, wigless woman. "What? I have a brain. And I'm a Harrow. I understand devious deeds." Xandie's grandmother ran a hand through her salt-and-pepper, short-cropped hair.

This was one of the few times Xandie had seen her wig-loving grandmother without a colorful monstrosity upon her head. Elspeth looked almost naked without her wig.

"Do you have a copy?" David cleared his throat. "I mean of the will, not the treasure map."

Elspeth raised an eyebrow in obvious surprise at the frantic undertones in his voice.

"I'm just concerned about my job is all. I'd like to know who's paying me or if I even have a job left." David shifted his grip on the lawyer. "Let's get them back to the house. See if they need any medical help."

Xandie carefully helped Elspeth stand and let David and the lawyer pass them first.

"Did he seem a little more anxious about the will than he should be to you?" Elspeth hissed to her granddaughter as Colin followed them outside.

"A little. Maybe he *is* concerned about his job? Must be hard for an ex-soldier to get a regular job."

"You need to be more suspicious of people's motives."

"I see you found the lawyer." Clinton Reed and Herbert Hedgewater stepped forward as Elspeth and Xandie exited the summerhouse. "And looks like he had a midnight rendezvous." Clinton winked at Elspeth as the rest of the houseguests jogged over to them.

Elspeth pointed a finger at the ex-cop. "Watch that smart mouth." An arc of electricity crackled around the tip of her manicured nails.

Breaking in before the squabble turned lethal, Xandie frowned at Clinton. "Weren't you supposed to check the summerhouse?"

"I saw the tree and figured no one could have gotten in. I didn't bother to try. The door was locked, anyway." Reed shrugged.

If he didn't try the door, how did he know someone had locked the summerhouse?

Elspeth was right. She needed to get her suspicions on, and Clinton Reed was the poster boy of suspicious behavior.

ELEVEN

"She's milking the drama for all she's worth." Lila sneered at her grandmother, now draped across the couch in the games' room with her cronies hovering nearby.

"At least we know where she is." Holly shrugged. "She could disappear, and then we'd have no idea what Elspeth-caused mayhem was headed our way."

"I'm glad I don't have to arrest her again." Braun grimaced. "Mom refused to cook for a week after the last time. My attempt at honey buns broke Caleb's fang."

Everyone in the Braun clan had a sweet tooth, but anything connected to honey sent bears crazy. Xandie could imagine Caleb gnawing desperately on Zach's over-baked honey bun.

"I'm glad your mom, Marjorie, and Winifred are here to run herd on her." Xandie lowered her voice. "Did you find out any extra information on Reed?"

"I searched his room. Caleb and Riley searched the summerhouse and the lawyer's room again. Came up with nothing. But considering the reputation he has of underhanded dealings, I'm betting you're right about him kidnapping the lawyer and stealing the will and map."

"Is he a killer?"

Aggie wandered over to Xandie and Braun and overheard Xandie's question. "I assume you're talking about that worm, Reed? In the right situation, he'd definitely strike first and ask questions later. Watch him. He's dangerous if crossed."

Xandie hugged Aggie. "We will, don't worry. Besides, you have Elspeth and Colin duty. That's more dangerous."

Aggie pinched Xandie's cheeks. "You're cute. Speaking of Elspeth, she wants someone to read to her. Apparently, Holly has a lovely speaking voice."

"No. Way." Holly popped up next to Xandie, shaking her head wildly. "Never again. I swore the last time she threw the book at me, no more reading."

Lila bent over, chortling. "So funny. Elspeth had a sprained ankle, and Holly offered to read to her, except she has a habit of putting on a different voice for each character. Drove Elspeth batty to the point she snatched the book and threw it at Holly."

"I had a bruise for a week on my forehead. Right in the middle of it." Holly jabbed her head.

Aggie wrapped an arm around Holly's waist. "Now, now, banshee. It'll be fine. Don't you want dear old Elspeth kept quiet?" Aggie nodded suggestively at the prone Elspeth. "I'll protect you, sweetie." The bear guided Holly away. "I'm sure your cousins will scoot straight off to the library and pick something appropriate for you to read."

At least Holly would keep Elspeth occupied for a while. "We'll jump right on that, Aggie." And she'd search the library for the missing journal at the same time. Xandie blew a kiss goodbye to Zach and dragged Lila out of the games' room.

"Why so eager to volunteer us? We've been slaving this whole weekend as it is."

"Because, dear Lila, Henry Hedgewater confirmed there *is* a journal penned by the murdered Sarah."

"Murder confirmed? Not a lovelorn suicide?"

"Hedgewater confirmed Abigail's version of the story. I guess the other rumor placed the captain in a better light than that of the murderer, so that's what the family ran with over the years."

"The sleuthing Librarian has a sniff of the trail. Then off we go snark hunting."

Ignoring Lila's antics, Xandie opened the door of the library. For once, Abigail wasn't in evidence.

"Here's my game plan." Xandie pointed to a small book-case of popular fiction. "Find something exciting for Elspeth to obsess over while I look for the journal." Abigail lived and breathed the books in the library, so it was kind of nice to search without her hovering behind them.

Xandie took one side of the room and worked methodi-cally through the first bookcase. It didn't take long, since most of the books sat packed in boxes already. "Abigail's already sorted a lot of the books. If there'd been a journal or an ancient portion of the stolen map in any of those books in the boxes, she'd have found it."

"Eureka." Lila held up a book.

"You found the journal?"

"Ah, no. I found the perfect book for Elspeth. *Crime and Punishment.*" Lila cackled, a pale imitation of her grandmother.

Elspeth and Lila had more in common than her cousin wanted to admit. Poking the metaphorical bear was definitely an Elspeth trait. "You're taking your life in your hands, but it's your funeral."

"Go out in a blaze of glory, I say." Lila hoisted the book over her head and yodeled a victory chant as she capered out the door.

"Can't choose your family." Shaking her head, Xandie continued her search. There were six bookcases left if she disregarded the multitude of boxes that lay haphazardly planted around the room. But still, who knew how long she had before Abigail arrived back in the library. "A needle in a haystack. A little help would be nice." She missed her own Library. By now, the Great Library of Alexandria would have floated the right book into her sweaty little hands.

"Ask and you shall receive." Colin nosed the door open and trotted in. His tail closed it behind him.

"I thought you were keeping an eye out for Elspeth?"

Colin nosed a book on its side and sneezed, dust and pug nose goo flying everywhere. "It's swords drawn for the baker and my girl. I choose not to stay in curse range."

"I don't blame you. Can you sniff out a journal written by a long dead pirate's wife?"

"Kid, I'm willing to give anything a go if you feed me."

Xandie blew Colin a kiss. "A kitchen trip if you give it a go and a special dinner cooked by Lila if you find the journal."

"Tally-ho." Colin surged forward as fast as his little pug legs could carry him. Nose down, he snuffled along the bookcases.

"Anything?"

"Smells like dust and trees so far. Never fear, doll face. Colin's on the prowl."

Xandie sagged against the bookcase. No offense to

Colin, but so far, all she'd seen the dog sniff was his next snack. The odds were not in her favor.

"Xandie?"

Colin's confused tones broke through Xandie's musings.

"What's wrong? Sniffer not working?"

"Something is in the way of my sniffer." Colin scooted back to Xandie and shivered against her leg.

Xandie inhaled as the wispy woman from the other night hovered near the last bookcase, next to where Xandie found the passage. "Sarah Hedgewater, I assume?"

The wispy figure bobbed up and down.

"I asked for a little help, I suppose, but I didn't expect a ghost with a murderous hatred for the Hedgewater family to help me."

The chin of the ghost pointed down as a wispy finger jabbed at a shelf in the bookcase.

"Okay, you want me to look there?" Xandie pried Colin off her leg and edged up next to Sarah. The air chilled around her, and goosebumps prickled Xandie's skin. She reached out and touched the book. "This one?" The chill grew more intense. "A game of hot and cold, I guess."

She let her hand drift over each book until she'd almost reached the end of the shelf. The surrounding air warmed as the ghost's wispy form slowly dissipated. Xandie stared at the woman's sad face. With an audible pop, she disappeared completely. The ghost's sadness flowed through Xandie. Knowing Hedgewater history, shouldn't Sarah have been angry? Drawing the leather-bound book out, Xandie cradled it in her hands as she moved back to Colin.

"I knew it was on that shelf. I'd already sniffed it out," Colin grouched. "Suppose you're gonna renege, now the ghost helped you."

"Never, Colin. A deal is a deal. Lila will cook you a meal fit for a princely pug."

"You're my favorite, kid. What did we get?"

Xandie opened the book, titled *A Piratical History*. But a few chapters in, the insides of the book were hollowed out and a small journal nestled inside. "Sarah's journal."

The sound of a large object grating against stone had Xandie slapping the book shut. A red-faced Abigail Berry sighed heavily as she stepped out of the passageway into the library and moved the bookcase back over the passage entrance.

Colin's yip of shock froze Abigail as she realized she wasn't alone. She raised a hand to her heart. "Xandie, you scared me. I wasn't expecting anyone to be here."

"We're equal then. I wasn't expecting you to come out of a hidden passage."

"Oh, that." Abigail waved at the bookcase. "Hidden passages riddle this place."

"Where does it lead?"

"Just downstairs." Abigail dismissed the question.

"This is downstairs. How much farther can we go?"

Abigail nibbled her lip. "You can't tell anyone, okay?"

Xandie shook head straight away. "No deal. I'm a duly appointed Point Muse Deputy, plus a Librarian, *and* I'm dating the police chief. He gets to veto any secret pacts I make."

Abigail sagged and came forward, dragging an old yellowed torn paper out of her pocket. "I found this going through the books. I think it's the portion of the map that's missing."

Peering at the faded scribbles on the map, Xandie's eyebrows shot up. "How does that explain the hidden passage?"

"This used to be Captain Hedgewater's library. The passage goes down to an old-fashioned, dirt floor wine cellar. There're old barrels of wine down there. I thought there might be another secret passage that would lead me to the treasure."

"But you need the clue and the other piece of the map, don't you?"

"You're right." Abigail threw her hands into the air. "I didn't sign the contract or pick up the clue. Thought it was all nonsense until I found this. I've been looking at it, and I think it's a map showing a path around Hedgewater's booby-traps."

"Since Henry confirmed your theory that the captain killed Sarah after she took a piece of his map, I'm pretty sure it isn't nonsense."

Abigail stiffened, all color drained from her face, and a hand tightened around the map. "He did? I knew it. All those stories. Poor woman."

"What stories and where did you hear them?"

"Just around." She spotted the book in Xandie's hand. "Light reading? I don't think I've cataloged that yet."

"This?" Xandie held the book up but refrained from spilling what she'd found inside. "I figured since we're all looking for a pirate treasure, I should read up on their exploits."

"Good idea. Bring it back when you're done, and I can add it to my list.". "Now that you know my nefarious plans to find the treasure, do you plan on denouncing me with suitable dramatic flair?"

"Drama is more my grandmother and Lila's thing, not mine."

"Well, I wouldn't say that exactly..." Colin stuttered to a stop when Xandie nudged him with a well-placed foot.

"What he means is I won't tell anyone about the map if you let me help you. These treasure hunters are pretty cutthroat when it comes to the Hedgewater treasure."

Abigail heaved a sigh of relief. "Of course. I need all the help I can get. Thanks, Xandie."

"No worries. I'd better get back to Elspeth before blood's shed." Xandie waved goodbye to Abigail and urged Colin out of the library. She made sure the door shut firmly behind them.

"Why did you lie?" Colin trotted behind Xandie.

"I didn't lie exactly. I just didn't tell her the whole truth. Considering there's a murderer on the loose, I think we should keep the journal a secret to everyone except the Harrows."

"And Brauns, and the dragon. She has fangs and claws and would be good in a fight."

"Yep, them too."

Xandie had the feeling the story of a murderous ghost was a convenient cover for a twisted and creative killer.

She just didn't know who yet...

TWELVE

"The treasure is mine. Mwahahaha." Elspeth villain-cackled, and the lights in the games' room flickered.

"Seriously? Could you speak any louder?" Lila sneered at her grandmother's antics.

"What? I've been practicing that laugh since Hedge-water died." Elspeth reared back, affronted, hand to her bony chest.

"Do we want it to get out that Abigail has the booby-trapped part of the map? Who knows what those treasure maniacs would do to the poor girl?" Winifred fussed with a pretty pink ribbon she'd attached to Petunia's collar.

"Petunia pretty. Pieces of eight. Need rest." The parrot launched into the air and flapped her wings wildly as she soared around the room.

"Oh hush, dear. You can rest if you want." Winifred tried to call the parrot to her hand, but Petunia refused.

"Find pieces of eight. Release us." The parrot flew to the mantelpiece and bobbed up and down. "Search for Sarah."

Xandie cocked her head and considered the bird.

Maybe there was more of a method to Petunia's mouthy madness than they realized. "The bird said search for Sarah. The only spot her name appears is the graveyard."

Lila snapped her fingers. "And her initials on the stone bench near the summerhouse."

"What about the journal, Alexandra? Is there any mention of the treasure in there?" Marjorie arched an exquisitely shaped dragon eyebrow at the Librarian.

Xandie suddenly felt like a student in the principal's office. She cleared her throat. "I made a cursory run through of the journal last night. But I need to read more in depth."

Holly giggled. "She fell asleep. I guess since there's only been one murder, it's hard to keep the sleuthing mojo going."

"Hey," Xandie protested. "No storm, no ghostly screams last night. The last few days just caught up with me, that's all."

Elspeth narrowed her eyes at her granddaughter. "Eyes on the prize, Meyers."

"Technically, Abigail found the map. It's *her* prize if she can unravel the booby-trapped map directions."

A high-pitched, unearthly scream echoed through the manor.

"Don't tell me Sarah, the ghost, is on a rampage again." Lila stood with hands over her head to protect her hair. "I refuse to deal with ghost ectoplasm. These locks are a ghost-free-product zone." She patted her luxurious brown curls.

"Let's find out." Xandie took off at a run and yanked the door open to find a shocked Clinton Reed.

"Did you hear that? You women okay?"

Reed didn't come across as the helpful type. More like the corrupt ex-cop eavesdropping on the women's conversation type. "Wasn't us. I think it came from upstairs."

"You okay, Xandie?" Braun and his twin brothers bolted inside the manor and skidded to a stop in front of the Harrows and Clinton Reed.

She pointed. "Upstairs."

The group ran upstairs, with Braun and his brothers in the lead. Xandie took the opportunity to admire the athletic ability of her bear shifter boyfriend.

"Wipe that drool off your face, this is serious." Lila kept pace next to Xandie as they took the stairs two at a time.

"I. Have. No. Clue. What. You're. Talking. About," Xandie puffed and almost ran into Zach's back when he stopped.

The police chief reached to steady Xandie without even looking. "I think we need to introduce you to cardio."

"Not if you want to have a girlfriend, you don't."

Xandie poked her head around Braun and stared at a prone Herbert, collapsed on the landing of the stairs, clutching his ankle.

Gloria ran out of her room, brassy blonde hair in old-fashioned rollers. "What happened? Who died?"

"No one. Your brother-in-law has twisted his ankle."

"One too many chasers for breakfast?" Gloria sneered at her Herbert.

"That's a lie. Someone pushed me. I swear it. I felt this hand on my back. Next thing I know, I fell down a couple of stairs and twisted my ankle. I grabbed the stair railing just in time. Otherwise I'd be the next Hedgewater dead."

Braun frowned and considered the stairs, then the hallway behind Hedgewater. "Did you see anyone?"

Herbert shook his head and then winced. "I felt wind on my neck and then the hand on my back..." He ground to a halt.

Poor Herbert looked like he wanted to say something but seemed almost too embarrassed to open his mouth.

"If you saw something, you need to tell us, Herbert," Xandie encouraged gently.

"Fine." Herbert blew a breath out. "Just as I hit the stairs, I thought I saw this wispy thing standing back, watching. I know you all think I'm a drunk, but this really happened. I'm not crazy."

"You're not mad. I think you saw Sarah Hedgewater." Xandie offered the visibly disturbed man a lifeline.

"A ghost tried to kill me?" Herbert shook his head. "I need to hit rehab again."

A gasp came from behind the group as Abigail climbed the stairs and joined Xandie. "Sarah's haunting you. I'm so sorry, that's horrible." Abigail wrung her hands in sympathy.

"What did I do to the ghost? We're related by marriage. Surely she'd be okay with a Hedgewater?"

"Captain Hedgewater killed her. Threw Sarah to her death after he caught her cheating," Abigail offered.

"Great. Killer ghost wants revenge on her murderer's family. Forget rehab, I need a drink."

"Don't be ridiculous, son. There's no such thing as ghosts." Henry held his hand out to his son and helped him stand on one leg.

"That old pirate, Horatio Hedgewater, killed the chick?" With his father's help, he hobbled to a small chair on the landing, collapsing into it with a deep sigh.

"Apparently, he murdered his wife, and she's still hanging around. But she didn't kill or injure any Hedgewaters."

"Why not?" Abigail rounded on Xandie. "Her husband

killed her for falling in love. That would make me vengeful."

"She stole a portion of the treasure map too. She's not entirely blameless." Xandie eyed Abigail meaningfully but held a hand up to forestall an argument. "That doesn't mean she deserved to die, of course. But there's something else." Xandie paused dramatically, waiting for someone to comment. "Really, people? The ghost, a spectral being without firm appendages. She can't push anyone. Whoever did this is flesh and bone and one of us."

A gaggle of protestations broke out, and Braun shushed them. "Everyone quiet down. Ghost talk aside, someone's died. Then we had a kidnapping and now we have an injury. Everyone needs to be careful. If you can pair up, that'd be better for everyone's safety."

"Except for the fact someone's a killer," Lila whispered to Xandie.

"May I suggest all guests head to the formal dining room?" Louisa indicated downstairs. "We've set up a breakfast buffet for those who wish to partake. A full stomach may settle some nerves for the moment." Without a smile, she spun around and stalked back downstairs.

"I thought she wasn't much of a cook?" Xandie questioned her baker cousin.

"Actually, she isn't a bad cook at all, and David's great at grilling meat. She just needed some direction is all." Lila rubbed her stomach. "I gotta eat me some scrambled eggs."

Xandie waved to Braun and followed her cousin to the dining room, the rest of the Harrows and assorted cronies tripping behind them.

Louisa stood at a set of doors opposite the games' room. A slightly stale odor emanated from the room.

"I don't think anyone's used this room in a while."

Harrison shuffled into the dining room alongside Xandie. "They haven't. Uncle Harry closed it down ten years ago. Either he took his meals in the games' room or his bedroom. He opened the dining room for the occasional family dinner just to lord it over us."

"I didn't see you in the hallway after someone pushed your brother."

He snorted. "Pushed...? Or tripped while in a drunken stupor? Herbert has a drinking problem. He's as much of a mess as the rest of us Hedgewaters."

Xandie smiled sweetly and pointed to a slightly damp spot on his pants legs. "That's not answering my question."

"Nosy, aren't you? To answer your question, even though it's none of your business, I checked the trees after the storm. We'd hate for a branch to drop on your head." He smirked and wandered off to the buffet table.

Clinton shoved past Xandie and loaded his plate with food. "I'm starving. Gotta keep my energy up for the treasure hunting."

Considering the energy he'd probably spent kidnapping the lawyer and stealing the map and will, no wonder he had a healthy appetite. "For curiosity's sake, where were you when Herbert took a tumble?"

Clinton sauntered up to Xandie, munching on toast. "You mean when the ghost pushed him? Don't you remember? I was right outside the games' room, making sure all you lovely women were safe." He put his toast-filled hand to his heart. "That's what law enforcement officers do. Protect and serve." He dropped the act and winked at Xandie.

"Does that include eavesdropping on private conversations?"

"Honey, everything's fair game when treasure hunting's

involved." Clinton leaned in. "Stay out of my way, Librarian."

"Or what?" No Harrow, or Meyers, responded well to threats.

"Do we have an issue here?" Braun stood next to Xandie and growled at Reed.

"No harm, no foul." Clinton raised his plate. "Just seeing if Miss Bookish wanted anything I had to offer."

Braun stepped in close, his massive bear chest and shoulders dwarfing the ex-cop's muscles-turned-to-paunch frame. "I suggest you leave Ms. Meyers alone and concern yourself with your own issues."

Clinton bared his teeth and casually placed his plate on the table. "What issues are those, bear?"

"The issue where I'll kick both your patooties if you don't sit on them," Elspeth hissed at the men and clapped her hands, flames erupting merrily over her knuckles. "I'm calling this the fist of fire. Isn't exactly original, but the oldies are goodies in my book. Now sit down." Elspeth raised her voice, and Colin planted his bottom down hurriedly.

Braun and Reed took longer to separate, but no one wanted to overrule Elspeth. Xandie dragged Braun over to a different spot on the large dining table. "He's just winding you up."

"He hates my family, and we don't exactly like him either." Braun leaned over and dusted a light kiss on Xandie's mouth. "He's dangerous. Be careful," he whispered.

Xandie dropped a flirty wink at Braun and whispered back, "Pretty sure he's the one who kidnapped the lawyer and knocked Elspeth out. He has the will and the treasure map."

Xandie watched as Clinton cozied up to Henry Hedgewater, their heads close together and their voices low. A shiver inched its way down her spine. She had a feeling whatever those treasure hunters were planning, it wouldn't end well.

Braun whistled. "I wouldn't want to be him when Elspeth finds out."

"When I found out what?" Elspeth loomed behind Braun, her fist of flame extended but not lit...yet.

Time for a distraction. "When you find out there's fresh tuna on the menu."

"Oh no," Elspeth wailed and bolted as fast as her short octogenarian legs would allow.

"Quick save, cousin, dear." Holly popped her head around Braun and clapped. "Masterful Elspeth distraction."

"Not fast enough." On the other side of Holly, Lila pointed to a tuna-gobbling pug.

Colin stopped gulping the tuna down and shuddered before tossing out an evil grin.

Xandie slapped hands over her and Braun's noses as a noxious green cloud wafted across the table.

When dealing with Harrows, best to be wary. Or in other words...

Be careful what you wish for.

THIRTEEN

"Fresh air." Xandie lifted her face to the weak sun and breathed deeply.

"I've never seen Aggie and Marjorie clear a room so quickly." Lila lounged on the stone bench next to Xandie, while Holly sat on a chair she'd dragged out of the summerhouse.

"I can't believe you let the housekeeper serve tuna. That's a Colin bomb waiting to go off." Holly wrinkled her nose. "It'll take weeks for the stink to disappear from that room."

"Honestly? I completely forgot to mention Colin has issues with seafood. At least Petunia missed the drama."

"Smart Petunia. Stinky dog." The parrot bobbed up and down on the back of the stone bench.

Xandie smoothed the feathers on top of the bird's head. "Petunia smart." She turned back to Sarah's journal and picked up where she'd left off earlier. The poor woman had been young and naïve when she'd married the captain. "Hedgewater hid his pirate life from Sarah. He kept her completely away from the pirate life and then deposited her on an isolated island, and she finally realized what kind of man she'd married."

"See." Lila pointed to the book. "It's a sign. You never know the measure of a guy until you marry him."

Holly rolled her eyes. "Please, we're still dateless because there's a decided lack of male talent in Point Muse that we haven't changed nappies for or watched eat their boogers. It puts a girl off."

"Zach's brothers are wonderful guys," Xandie protested.

"Case in point. Both Lila and I babysat those twin horrors. I'll never forget the makeup incident." Holly closed her eyes and shuddered. "I can still picture the traumatizing incident."

"Do I want to know?"

"Holly's fault, not mine. We looked after the twins and one of us..." Lila pointed to her cousin. "...bought some makeup. We were banned from wearing any, but she snuck some to practice with. The twins found it and painted themselves, the carpet, and the walls with it. Aggie wasn't pleased, and Elspeth had to quit her poker game to come and help us clean the mess. She made us pay in slave labor for a month."

"And gave us Vesuvius-sized pimples for a straight week."

Xandie sighed. "I shouldn't have asked, should I?"

"Growing up Harrow is traumatic. We all have issues." Holly sniffed.

"*And* back to the journal. Any other insights or clues?" Lila asked.

"Sarah hated her husband's job as a pirate. Apparently, one had killed her father. Combine that issue with months at sea and their marriage died."

Lila snorted. "Not to mention, her husband literally killed her."

"Throughout the journal, she talks about the kindness of her husband's business partner. Little things, like bringing treats for Petunia and books for her library." Xandie winced. "Pretty sad when toys for your bird and a book to read amounted to the best gifts she'd ever had."

"The chick had a sad life. Now let's get to the dirty bits." Lila waggled her eyebrows. "Let me guess, the boyfriend and present-giving guy are the same?"

"By the looks of it. Josiah Barnes features throughout the journal. She talks about his gift for numbers, how her husband blackmailed him into working for the pirate crew." Xandie looked up. "The *Blood Pearl* is the name of Hedgewater's ship."

"I'm not liking Hedgewater much." Holly grimaced. "I'd have run off too."

Xandie watched as the twin Hedgewaters and Gloria darted from the house to the graveyard. Looked like poor Herbert's ankle had miraculously healed itself. Odds were, they were treasure hunting. She spotted Abigail wandering around near the boathouse where the housekeeper and David stood in a whispered conversation. The eldest Hedgewater and Reed had disappeared. Elspeth and her cronies had installed themselves in the kitchen, making mock-tails, and Zach and his brothers were wandering somewhere around the island.

"Earth to Xandie. What's wrong?"

Shaking off her thoughts, Xandie smiled at her cousins. "Watching the treasure hunters and wondering what Henry Hedgewater and Reed have planned. Henry told me he knows exactly where the treasure is but because of the booby-traps, he can't get to it. And Reed eavesdropped on our conversation about Abigail having Sarah's piece of the map."

"You're worried about her."

Xandie nodded at Lila. "She's a target, and I think greed will drive those two to do anything to get her bit of the map."

"So, you need to hurry and study the book. Maybe Sarah wrote something that will help Abigail find the treasure first," Holly pointed out.

"There *are* a few interesting things. Did you know Sarah had a child? A boy. She named him Josiah after his father."

"Oh, how sad." Holly wiped away a small tear. "Her son never knew his mother."

Xandie swallowed a lump that appeared in her throat. She'd had her mom back for a while now, but she knew what it felt like to grow up without a parent. "But she got her husband back. It says in the journal the captain had an especially large treasure haul, and he hid it from prying eyes. There were loads of caves under the cliffs near the boathouse. He waited for the tides and floated an old wreck and sank the boat with his treasure on it. Laid booby-traps and wrote the map. Even had a couple of loyal servants to help."

"Let me guess. He rewarded them by killing them, so they'd never speak about the treasure?"

Xandie agreed with Lila. "Pretty much. From what I can gather, most of the servants were ex-pirates and pretty feral. Sarah had a handful of her own servants she'd brought out from England who she trusted."

Holly leaned forward, eagerness written across her face. "This story's getting interesting. Keep going."

"He had a passageway in the library where he hid things.

She waited until his last voyage and stole the portion of the map containing the booby-traps. She mentioned a secret mission her loyal servants carried out. And she set up clues for her son to follow in case she died, then she hid the journal."

"What about the baby?" Lila echoed Holly's enthusiasm.

"She hid the pregnancy behind big skirts, and her servants never breathed a word. The baby came early, and she gave birth out in the summerhouse. Josiah Sr. arrived to take them away. But she refused. Then a servant spotted the captain's ship on the horizon. So, Sarah made Josiah take the baby and swore she'd follow them. She wanted to hide the map first. Sarah hid the map in the library right under Hedgewater's nose. But by then, he'd arrived home. She gave her servants last-minute instructions, then fled."

Holly gasped, hand to mouth. "He found her, didn't he?"

"Mistress gone." Petunia wailed and flapped her wings in a flurry.

"It's okay, Petunia," Xandie soothed. "He caught her on the cliffs. Accused her of stealing his map and of having an affair. They struggled, she hit him on the head, and he shoved her off the cliff. He came to with no idea what had happened. He looked for the treasure for the rest of his life. Apparently, he couldn't even remember where he'd hidden it. The rock did some serious damage to his brain."

"How do you know all that if Sarah died?" Lila frowned.

"The servants." Xandie turned the book around to show them the difference in writing. "Sarah's script is neat and flowing. The writing at the end is more like a heavy scrawl."

"And?"

"Even though the family never recovered Sarah's body, her loyal servants erected a monument in the graveyard for her. Besides, Josiah Sr. and the baby disappeared, so Hedgewater couldn't find them. The servants hid the journal and then disappeared themselves. And that's the whole sordid story in a nutshell."

Lila suddenly broke in. "I've just realized something. Given all the relatives running around this place, Hedgewater must have remarried some time after Sarah died. Otherwise how else could he have begat so many family members?"

Before anyone could respond to Lila's comments, Petunia took flight, flapping over their heads. "Release us. Find pieces of eight," she squawked again before heading toward the house.

"Ever get the feeling that feathered menace knows more about this whole treasure thing than we realize?"

Xandie snorted at Lila's comment. "I think there's an entire list of people who know more than we do. And Clinton Reed tops the list."

Lila grabbed the journal and slid it back into its secret hiding place in the book on pirate history. She flicked a few pages over and covered the hollowed-out area with the journal and pretended to read.

"Well, Ms. Meyers. I'm flattered I'm on any list of yours." Clinton smirked at Xandie. "Voices carry here. I heard you mention I'm on your list. Suspect list, I take it?"

"I definitely think you're capable of strong-arm tactics when you want something." Xandie glared at the intrusive man. She understood why the Braun clan hated him. Something about him rubbed people the wrong way.

"I take that as a compliment." He pointed to Lila's book

on pirates. "Light reading. Are you entering the treasure hunt?"

Lila bared her teeth in a parody of a smile. "Maybe? The lure of pirate gold makes for an exciting adventure."

Clinton sighed dramatically. "Alas, your hunt may be short-lived. There's a rumor someone found the site of the treasure."

"Did this rumor come from your new partner, Henry Hedgewater? Will he get twenty percent of the treasure like his brother? And what about the booby-traps?"

Clinton smiled lazily. "Partnerships are made to be broken. As for the booby-traps, I've solved that issue."

He'd discovered Abigail's portion of Captain Hedgewater's map. "You have a good luck rabbit's foot you're fondling?" Xandie arched an eyebrow.

"Ha. Good one." Clinton slapped his leg in mirth. "Maybe I *am* that lucky." He nodded at the boathouse. "But your little book friend might not be as lucky as I am. You should check on her." With a dip of his imaginary hat, he wandered away.

Xandie waited for him to disappear out of sight, then jumped up. "Take the journal back to our room and see if you can find anything else. I have to make sure Abigail's okay." Without waiting for an answer, Xandie bolted down to the boathouse.

Louisa and David had disappeared. No sign of them outside the boathouse. But unfortunately, no sign of Abigail either.

"Abigail? Are you okay? Can you hear me?" Xandie yelled, with hands cupped, but she heard nothing. She peered along the path that led to the dock, but it remained empty. Xandie shuffled closer to the side of the pathway that looked over the edge of the island's small beach. Lots of small caves set into the cliff and footprints all over the sand, but no Abigail. Xandie caught sight of Clinton on the top of the cliffs overlooking the beach and the caves. She grimaced when he waved mockingly at her.

The way he stood showboating and mocking her niggled at Xandie's nerves.

A muffled shout distracted Xandie, and she spun back to the boathouse. Someone had wedged a shovel under the door's handle. Xandie grabbed it and flung it to the ground.

The door swung open, and a frazzled Abigail flew out, collapsing on the ground at Xandie's feet.

"Someone locked me in the boathouse. I didn't think anyone would find me." Abigail shuddered. "It's like a dank cave in there. Smells like men's sweat socks."

"That's it." Xandie gently took hold of Abigail's arm and hoisted her to her feet.

Abigail stared quizzically at Xandie. "What's it?"

"I know where Captain Hedgewater hid his treasure, but unfortunately, so does Clinton Reed."

Just a matter of time before the next treasure hunter's body turned up...

FOURTEEN

"The dark hole of my heart hides what you seek with ebb and flow. Beware treacherous traps that lead the seeker astray. X marks the spot. My fortune found."

"Poetic, I guess." Lila faked a gag. "If one likes second-rate pirate poetry."

"That's the whole clue to where Captain Hedgewater hid his treasure."

Elspeth's eyes widened. "You know where the treasure is, don't you?"

"'X marks the spot. My fortune found.' Yes, I know exactly where it is."

And Clinton and Henry knew, too. They needed Sarah's portion of the map to avoid the traps. And she bet they had it after Reed's eavesdropping. Xandie turned to Abigail. "You need to check and make sure Sarah's portion of the map is safe." Didn't hurt to see if her hunch about Reed stealing the map was correct.

Abigail nodded and took off at a run.

Waiting for the woman to disappear, Xandie spun and

spoke to her friends and family gathered in the kitchen. "It doesn't matter if we work out where the captain hid his treasure originally. Sarah and her loyal servants moved the entire thing. Even if Reed and Hedgewater avoid the booby-traps and find the area where it was buried, there's nothing there anymore. Only Sarah knows, and she took it to the grave."

Lila held up a piece of paper. "Not necessarily."

Holly bounced up and down in her chair like an excited child. "We found something in the journal."

Elspeth crowed. "I knew it'd be worth putting money into your education."

Winifred looked confused. "What money?"

Ignoring her daughter, Elspeth waved the girls on like a queen presiding over her court. "Carry on, my favorite granddaughters."

"We flicked through the book and noticed some of Sarah's writing had a different pressure to it. Darker than the rest."

"Maybe just her quill? Or whatever she used to write with then."

"That's what we thought. Until we noted all the darker words."

Holly dramatically swung to face Lila. "Cousin, you do the honors."

"Noble of you, since I have the paper." Lila read aloud, "'My revenge lies below. Stolen from a cruel master. Sit a spell and rest where I found my love. The one who lit my stone-cold heart. The key's in plain sight. Grieve my rest and trace my name to open the way. Unlock the path to seek the fortune. Well-hidden with love's touch. My blessings upon you.'"

Marjorie Penne snorted on a puff of smoke. "That's as

clear as mud. Why can't people speak plainly? *I buried the treasure here.*"

"She had to speak in riddles in case Captain Hedgewater found her journal. I suspect she probably hoped her lover or son would find the treasure if she didn't make it back to them."

Winifred waved a hand in the air like an inquisitive student. "Where do we start?"

Xandie smiled slowly. "I have an idea."

"You lied to me." Abigail stood framed in the doorway, fists closed and face flaming red.

"I didn't lie. I just didn't tell you I found Sarah's journal."

"Lied by omission." Abigail spat the words out. "You're supposed to help me, not stab me in the back."

"Hey. Calm down." Xandie held up a hand.

"No!" Abigail yelled the word and stepped into the kitchen. "You have no clue what I've sacrificed. This was my grandfather's dream. I can't let him down." Abigail sagged into a chair at the kitchen table and dropped her head into her hands, groaning.

"You didn't come here to value books, did you?" Xandie kept her voice low and sympathetic. Abigail was way too upset for this just to be about a missing journal.

"Finding the Hedgewater treasure. My grandfather's dream."

"The same man who died before you came here?"

Abigail raised her head. "My grandfather, Jason Berry."

"The bookseller?"

"Valuer of printed works." Abigail smiled with a wobble. "He came across the legend of Sarah Hedgewater. I think he felt a connection with the story. He became obsessed with finding the treasure and making a difference.

He contacted Harry, suggested he needed evaluation of the library in case anything expensive lay in the collection. The Hedgewaters are dirt poor, so he jumped at the idea of easy cash."

"And then your grandfather died."

"I promised I would finish what he started. I won't let him down."

"Oh, sweetie." Winifred scooted over and grabbed Abigail in a tight hug. "We understand. We really do. But you're lucky Xandie wasn't raised a Harrow. She knows how to share." Winifred beamed at the room. "She's the best of us."

"Geez, thanks, Mom." Holly pouted for a moment but then let the act drop. "She isn't wrong."

"I guess I could share." Elspeth grouched with only a brief twitch to her lips.

"That means you're in. Now dish where you think we should start, Xandie," Lila encouraged her cousin.

"We'll help you." Xandie patted Abigail's hand. She couldn't help but feel the Hedgewater treasure had obsessed more than one family.

"Oh, I forgot. Someone broke into my room and searched it. They have Sarah's portion of the map." Abigail grimaced. "It slipped my mind when I heard you talking about Sarah's journal."

"Clinton Reed and Henry Hedgewater teamed up. Reed overheard us talking about the map this morning. It's our fault he found out about Sarah's map." Xandie smirked. "Then again, they won't find the treasure, anyway. A very smart woman moved it and left us clues to follow." Xandie tapped the journal.

"I take it, dear Alexandra, you have an idea where to start our hunt?" Marjorie ran a silver claw across the top of the journal. "Dragons love a good hunt." The elderly dragon matriarch bared teeth that looked a tad sharper and longer than before.

"It's in the words." Xandie read the first line. "'My revenge lies below.' Obviously, that means the treasure is buried somewhere. 'Stolen from a cruel master.' That's Hedgewater." Xandie paused. "Everyone with me?" She waited for their assent, then continued, "'Sit a spell and rest where I found my love.' I'm positive that refers to the carved stone bench near the summerhouse. The next bit, I have no clue about. 'Who lit my stone-cold heart. The keys are engraved in plain sight.'" Xandie looked up. "That's the important part. Engraved in plain sight. Remember those initials with numbers and letters we found scored into the stone bench?"

"The keys in plain sight." Lila slapped her forehead. "The initials on the stone lead to the next clue."

Xandie cleared her throat. "Actually, I think she's giving us the exact directions we need to navigate the caves where she hid the treasure." She sat back, pleased with herself.

"And the rest?" Abigail sat up, eyes shining.

"The rest we take step-by-step. First, the stone bench. Two of us casually stroll out in a little while and find the directions while the others repair to the games' room for a brief lunch. Very casually. We can't let Clinton or anyone else get wind of what we're doing."

"And my son?" Aggie raised an eyebrow at Xandie. "Do you plan on telling him the plan?"

Xandie snorted. "Like I could hide it from him. But he knows when to let things play out if the situation's fluid."

Elspeth weighed in. "Let the younger ones take point. Xandie has a smart head on her shoulders. Oldies will be support crew this time around." Xandie's grandmother nodded regally. "We shall remove ourselves to the games' room. Xandie and Abigail can go to the bench while Lila and Holly make our lunch." Elspeth picked up a slumbering Colin and drifted out of the room, an elegant grand dame in a fluorescent green wig.

"Got to give it to her. The old girl's got style." Lila waved Xandie and Abigail out of the kitchen. "Get going. Treasure needs hunting down."

Nodding, Xandie opened the kitchen door and wandered out, Abigail following her. The kitchen door to the outside opened at the back of the house. Taking their time, the girls strolled around the house in the direction of the summerhouse.

"This is exciting," Abigail murmured. "My family's dream for such a long time, almost in touching distance."

"Don't count your pirate gold yet." Xandie stole a glance at the graveyard. Cemeteries weren't her favorite place to visit, especially since the zombie dragon incident a while ago. But something about Sarah's empty monument called to her.

"Xandie? You okay?" Abigail stared worriedly at the Librarian. "You kind of blanked out for a moment."

Xandie forced a smile. "Sorry. Thinking about the monument to poor Sarah. There wasn't even a body to bury, even if there had been no way her lover and son could visit the island and mourn her. Hedgewater would have killed them."

"They remembered her. Josiah Barnes did everything he could to keep Sarah alive in her son's memories."

"How do you know?" Xandie frowned. "They didn't even have the journal."

"My grandfather spoke to someone from the family. That's where he tracked down most of his information. He wanted to find the treasure and hand it back to Sarah's descendants. The treasure she died for is rightfully theirs."

Abigail's face glowed with enthusiasm. Xandie wanted to agree with her. The Hedgewaters were truly horrible people, but didn't they at least deserve a portion of the treasure as well? Their obsession with it had destroyed their lives just as Sarah's had been. "I'm not sure on the laws and such about discovering treasure on someone's land. We may have to give up a percentage to the government and the family."

"We'll see about that." Abigail shot Xandie a determined look. "But we need to find the first initial. Lead on, Librarian."

Strolling toward the summerhouse, Xandie glanced around. Reed and his partner had disappeared, probably still trying to get into the caves below where Clinton had waved to Xandie. Low tide wasn't until tomorrow. Until then, they were plain out of luck. The younger Hedgewaters had progressed over to the other side of the small island where a wooded area stood. The housekeeper and the caretaker had walked off in a secret huddle. Xandie had a sneaking suspicion why the mismatched duo seemed so close. But she'd keep quiet until the treasure situation unfolded more.

"Isn't that your boyfriend?" Abigail pointed down to the dock where Braun and his deputy brothers stood gesturing animatedly.

Xandie frowned as she sat on the carved stone bench, adjusting her seat as the cold of the stone bit into her nether regions. "He doesn't look too happy. I wonder what's happened?"

Abigail dismissed Xandie's concerns with a wave of a hand. "Considering this cursed place, it could be anything.

Let's get our directions and skip back inside, start working the next clue."

"Good point." Xandie trotted out her old favorite movement and pretended her laces were untied. Bending over, she traced a hand over the initials. S.H. followed by L.2. Straightening, Xandie smiled at Abigail, pretending to relax against the bench. "Got it."

"What is it?"

"S.H. L.2."

"S.H. is obviously Sarah Hedgewater, but what does L.2. mean?"

"We'll work it out when we get back to the house. We still need to puzzle out the last line. 'Who lit my stone-cold heart.'" Xandie patted Abigail's shoulder. "This is a team effort. Don't worry. Everything will be fine."

Except for the vengeful villain stalking the house, everything was great...

FIFTEEN

"Someone doesn't want us to leave the island." Xandie stood at the top of the path down to the boathouse, but the caretaker's voice carried to where she stood clearly enough.

"Sarah Island is run down. Isn't it possible you missed the problems with the skiffs? The boathouse?"

"The house might be run down, but not my boathouse. I'm not an idiot or incompetent. I'm telling you, this was deliberate. I checked them yesterday, and everything looked fine."

"And when did you see the island's cruiser last?"

The sound of a meaty thump accompanied by cursing made it plain to Xandie that David wasn't happy with her police chief boyfriend's questions.

"Spying again, Meyers?"

Xandie squeaked as Zach Braun's youngest brother, Riley, loomed over her. She flung out a hand and whacked the bear shifter in the stomach.

"Ouch. Why did you do that, Xandie?"

"Because you scared me. You know how I react to surprises."

Riley Braun was the youngest of the Braun brothers by five minutes. The twins were of a slim build compared to Zach. Although they were all bear shifters and built on the larger size, anyway. Riley shared sandy brown hair and blue eyes with the rest of the Braun clan. But unlike his no-nonsense, eldest brother, Riley had a devious streak and liked to tease the Harrow women. Especially his brother's girlfriend.

Riley rubbed his stomach and winced. "Shelving books must be hard work. Your hit has power."

Ignoring Riley's whining, Xandie stared at Braun and David. "What's happened? Tell me there wasn't another body found floating around out there."

"Not yet." Riley rubbed his chin. "Might as well tell you, since Zach probably will, anyway. The island's cruiser. The boat everyone came over on. It's missing, and the little skiffs in the boathouse are damaged."

"No way off the island? What about the boats that brought you over?"

"Point Muse fishermen."

"We're all stuck here with a murderer? That's great. Harrow luck strikes again."

"Not exactly." Zach slipped in next to Xandie and wound an arm around her waist. "Don't spread it around, but I have a satellite phone. I can call for backup or a boat anytime I need to."

"And David swears he checked the boathouse yester-day. Someone stole the cruiser and sabotaged the skiffs."

Braun nodded at Xandie. "Caleb, Riley, and I stood watch last night, but this is a big Island. It would've been easy for someone to sneak out."

"I heard something when I patrolled downstairs and felt

wind on the back of my neck, but when I turned around, no one was there."

"I told you last night, Riley. There is no ghost."

Xandie bit her lip. "Um, there kind of is a ghost."

"Really?" Braun's eyebrows rose in surprise.

"Sarah Hedgewater. I've seen her and so have a few others. But I don't think she's a murderer. I think you need to look at Clinton Reed."

"The guy Dad hated?" Riley asked his brother.

"Yeah. He's definitely capable of murder."

"Not to mention theft and kidnapping," Xandie added. "I'm sure he kidnapped Emmett and Elspeth and stole Abigail's portion of the Hedgewater map."

"Riley, tell Caleb to concentrate on Reed. You and I will patrol the house and grounds in shifts."

Riley nodded and headed back to the house.

Braun rubbed his forehead. "I knew this weekend with Elspeth and her cronies wouldn't end well. Add one Harrow, let alone multiple Harrows, and you get mayhem."

Xandie winced and linked her arm with Zach's. "I can't deny chaos loves our family. It's not like we *want* to stumble across bodies."

"I know."

Xandie made commiserating noises. "It's a trial being a boyfriend to the Librarian. I'm sure you're earning good karma points somewhere in the world."

Braun smirked. "The Librarian isn't the issue. It's the chaos-causing relatives." He tugged Xandie closer and drifted a gentle kiss over her lips, deepening it for a moment before easing back. "Deputy, let's get you inside. It's late, and you need to be on your game when you hunt down the treasure and the killer."

Xandie had filled Zach in earlier about Sarah's journal

and the clue. He'd asked her to be careful, but she had Harrow genes and trouble followed like a shadow.

"One of us will be around, so if you have an issue, yell."

They stepped inside the house, and Braun ushered Xandie upstairs.

"You know, you don't need to walk me to my door. I'm a big girl," Xandie whispered.

"You're a body magnet. It's safer for all of us if I do," he whispered back.

Rolling her eyes, Xandie blew Braun a kiss and stepped inside the attic room she shared with her cousins. Thankfully, the moon shone tonight. At least she wouldn't fall over while getting into bed. Quickly changing into her long sleep pants with *Librarians shelve it better* stenciled across the top, Xandie slid under the covers and closed the eyes, waiting for sleep to take her.

And waited.

And waited.

Slapping the covers, Xandie cracked one eye open. Only to spot a flash of wispy fog drifting across her bed. "Are you kidding, Sarah? It's late. And Braun will *not* be happy if I get up again," Xandie hissed at the ghost and froze as Lila snorted and rolled over in her sleep.

The fog with the woman's face made another chilling pass over Xandie's bed. As the ghost turned to make another pass, Xandie held up a hand and flipped the covers off. "If Braun asks, you get to do the explaining."

The chill in the room lightened as the wisp bobbed up and down like a woman amused.

"Laugh it up, ghost." Xandie stood and walked to the attic door. "You're the boss."

The fog flew through the door and downstairs to the main floor of the manor.

Xandie lifted her phone. Measly light emanating from the screen at least ensured she wouldn't trip over obstacles and wake the house. "Come on, Sarah. Where are we going?"

A flickering light appeared under the door of the games' room. "Okay, that's a pretty obvious clue." The fog flew through the door. Xandie followed but opened the door instead of giving herself a headache. She gasped softly as she stepped inside. She'd forgotten Sarah had claimed the room first.

A roaring fire flamed brightly in the fireplace. Beautiful paintings in ornate frames covered the walls. Burgundy-colored velvet couches were placed invitingly around the stone hearth. Thick, warm rugs covered the floor and an ornate piano sat in the corner. A blazing crystal chandelier hung from the center of the room. At the end near the windows sat a large wooden desk.

The same desk a real-life Sarah Hedgewater now sat bent over, scribbling into the same journal Xandie had just pored over. "Oh, Sarah." The wispy fog drifted over to her own body and hovered, trailing a hand over her forehead.

"You wanted me to see you as you were?"

The past Sarah eased back from the desk and closed her journal. She stared out the window, her hazel eyes dreamy, auburn hair trailing down her back in curls. And a hand rested gently on her curved stomach.

"You're pregnant with Josiah." Xandie fought the tears filling the back of her throat. So sad to see the soon-to-be mother dreaming of the future she'd never have.

Sarah's ghost shifted to Xandie and let her hand trail across Xandie's tears.

Xandie had the feeling Sarah hadn't shown her this image to make her sad, but then why?

The other Sarah sighed and stood. Walking to the window, she stared out. "You'll always know how much you were loved and wanted. I have no care for material wealth. I have seen how it corrupts. But you will always have love. No matter what might happen to me."

No matter what happens? "She knew her husband would kill her. That's

why she gave her son to her lover. Sarah knew what her husband would do to her."

Pregnant Sarah slowly turned around and stared at the space where Xandie stood. "The treasure consumed and corrupted my husband and his crew. They care for nothing but those pieces of eight. And have even less care for the blood spilled to achieve their wealthy dreams."

Petunia flew into the room, squawking, "Pieces of eight. Cursed. Cursed."

Sarah held out a hand, and the parrot landed gently, rubbing a feathered head against her mistress. "That's right, my pretty girl. Cursed, and we want no part of it for our family. Leave it for another to find. Someone a long time away from us." Sarah lifted her head and gave a watery smile to the room. "Some nights, I would wait for the servants to sleep. I would take a hidden passage and meet my love in this very room. We'd dance in front of the stony hearth and warm ourselves with our love."

Xandie blinked rapidly as Sarah's words registered. *The next clue, the stone hearth.* Making a snap decision, Xandie stepped forward and spoke to the Sarah from the past. "We found a journal and the first clue. We'll make sure you won't be forgotten."

"Don't let the treasure corrupt. Too much blood and tears spilled. No more. I don't want the blood on my soul any longer."

The fire snapped out. The warm interior bled back into the threadbare games' room Xandie knew now. Human Sarah disappeared, and Petunia took flight, landing on Xandie's shoulder. "Hecate's kneecaps, Petunia. Is there something you want to tell me?" Ghost Petunia and real Petunia were the same bird.

"Spoilers," Petunia cackled, sounding suspiciously like a twin of Elspeth's. Sarah's manor, full of surprises.

"Release us," Petunia squawked and lifted into the air, hovering next to ghost Sarah.

The wisp of a ghost seemed to brighten for a second before dissipating into the air.

"Don't worry, Sarah and Petunia. The Harrows have got your backs."

"Ms. Meyers? Is there a problem?" A dressing-gown-clad Louisa, with unbound auburn hair, stared perplexed at Xandie.

"Sorry." Xandie winced. "I couldn't sleep and then I heard Petunia." She pointed to the ceiling where the bird now performed lazy figure eights in the air.

"Houdini of a bird. She always gets out of the cage even when she's locked in." Louisa shook her head in amazement.

The housekeeper seemed much more approachable in her dressing gown. Not wound so tight.

"Come on, Petunia. Let's have our midnight snack." Louisa paused and looked back at Xandie. "Hot chocolate nightcap?"

"Now you're speaking my language." Xandie caught up to Louisa, and they entered the kitchen together.

"I have a bit of a sweet tooth, so when I can't sleep, I fix myself a hot chocolate. Petunia normally keeps me company." Louisa bustled around, getting the makings for hot chocolate together.

"I'll admit I'm addicted to hot chocolate. I'm happy to drink it at any time."

"This madhouse can take some getting used to. All the creaks and groans can make it hard to settle down."

"And the ghost." Xandie waited for a reaction. *Laughter or shock?* But the housekeeper kept her face as solid as a rock. "You know about Sarah, don't you?"

Louisa placed a hot chocolate on the table in front of Xandie and grabbed her own. "Yes. I know Sarah haunts the island." Louisa's hazel eyes twinkled. "She showed herself within twenty-four hours of me being on the island. Petunia adores her."

"You don't seem concerned."

Louisa smiled. "It's a little-known fact, but I'm addicted to ghost hunter shows. And she's friendly. She would never hurt me."

Xandie snorted. "She doesn't mind interrupting a girl's sleep."

"I find her and Petunia comforting." Louisa smiled fondly at the bird, perched on the back of the kitchen chair. "They've become family."

Xandie went for shock value. "I guess it's nice to have another female around, even if it's a ghost. There's only so much support a son can give his mother."

Louise's cup paused halfway to her mouth, the only reaction she gave Xandie. "I forgot you're the Librarian and a sleuth."

"I happened to catch a glimpse of a photo in David's room at the boathouse. A young man and an older woman. David tried to hide it by turning the frame face down, so it took me a while to work it out. Mother and son."

"Very perceptive."

"My family would deny that accusation vehemently." Xandie winked. "Why did both of you move here?"

"David left the military and found it hard to get a job. I'd been looking for something different and found Sarah Island. I enquired and Hedgewater's lawyer informed me the owner needed a live-in caretaker and a housekeeper. We both took this opportunity to get to know the family better. And here we are."

Everything Louisa said made sense, so why did Xandie feel the housekeeper still hid something else?

Louisa stood and washed her cup. "I hope you won't mention our relationship. I don't want the family sneering at David for taking a job with his mother."

Xandie took her cue and stood. "Hedgewaters in glass houses shouldn't throw stones."

"Excuse me?"

"No one gets my humor," Xandie grouched with a smile. "I don't think the family should comment when there are quite a few skeletons in their own closet."

"More than you know," Louisa murmured to herself, before standing and moving to the kitchen door. "Try to get some sleep. Goodness knows what tomorrow will bring us."

Xandie nodded her thanks and shuffled out the door. She watched as Petunia flew to the housekeeper's shoulder and nuzzled her like she'd nuzzled the human Sarah.

Louisa was right. Who knew what tomorrow would bring? Just as long as it wasn't another body...

SIXTEEN

"I tell you, someone's going to die today. I feel it in my banshee bones." Holly lounged on one of the threadbare couches that faced the softly glowing fire in the games' room.

"Have you had a vision?" Although Xandie didn't think her cousin was far off the mark. Her own sleuthing bones itched.

"Not yet, but then, with my Harrow blend of genes, who knows when this signal will come through to my death antenna."

"Makes you sound like a bug I need to squish." Lila shuddered. "Bugs are bad."

"Is it rest time already? I thought we were treasure hunting?" Elspeth stood framed in the games' room doorway, flaming red tresses flowing out behind her.

"Rocking the red hair, doll face." Colin trotted past Elspeth and plopped down in front of the fire.

"Red hair, just don't care." Elspeth twirled her long red wig locks coquettishly. Dropping the act, she glared at her granddaughters. "Now, no lollygagging. We need to find the treasure."

Aggie and Marjorie shoved past Elspeth and, like Lila and Holly, dropped to another couch.

"Yeah, these beds are lumpy. I need my big bear bed back." Aggie groaned and rubbed her hip.

Marjorie curled her lip. "I think I've overdosed on the Hedgewaters' lack of creature comforts. I miss my hoard. Wrap up this treasure and murder hunt, Librarian. Point Muse is calling."

"Yeah, the weekend is kind of stretching out to the weekday now. There's only so much my brownie, Hester, can cope with before she quits again."

"Turning on me, Lila?" Xandie mimed pulling a knife out of her back and then winced at her insensitive gesture. Since Harry Hedgewater died by stiletto to the back, it wasn't exactly politically correct to make fun of it.

"Where's lover boy and his brothers, kid? They on the killer's trail yet?" Colin rolled over and waggled his paws in the air, warming them in front of the fire.

"Zachy and the twins have headed out early." Aggie adjusted on the couch gingerly. "They heard a racket on the stairs this morning. Belonged to that real estate bimbo arguing with her husband. The boys raced out after that."

Winifred nodded. "Poor man. She's quite strident. Apparently, she hadn't realized her bracelet was only paste. She's very unimpressed. Told him to find the real stuff or sleep elsewhere, like another house."

"My sister-in-law has strong opinions about genuine diamonds. The more expensive, the more she wants." Herbert stood in the doorway, a crystal glass in one hand, the other hanging onto the door. He winked at the women and wavered on his feet for a moment.

"Been at the whiskey for breakfast, dear brother?" A sneering Harrison stood behind his brother.

Herbert raised a glass in a cheer to his sober sibling. "Have to do something while we wait for the good times to roll on."

"Quiet." Harrison shot an apologetic glance at the room. "He doesn't know what he says when he's under the weather."

"Say it plain, son. He's tanked. Got a skin full. Drunk." Aggie grunted.

"He has issues, that's all." Harrison yanked his brother aside and whispered ferociously to him.

Xandie spared the brothers any familial tension and let them off the hook. "It's low tide this morning. We know your dad and Reed will head to the caves at the bottom of the cliff to find Captain Hedgewater's treasure."

Harrison jerked and dropped his brother's arm.

Herbert drained his glass and bellowed honking laughter. "She's great. Dad and Reed have been sneaking around and she guessed the secret straight up. What a woman." The drunk twin pointed to Xandie. "She's my favorite."

"She gets that a lot," Lila murmured.

"Actually, I don't know where Father is. He left for his normal morning walk a few hours ago, but I haven't seen him since. Clinton looked for him for an hour or so but gave up and left for the tunnels."

"We got a problem, Library Girl." Colin rolled to his feet, his nose pointed straight at a tensed Holly.

The banshee's eyes wavered to silver instead of her normal Harrow amber, her head jerked and she shrieked. An undulating wail built up in the room and exploded out. Even the windows and doors rattled and creaked at the noise.

"Someone's dead." Colin ran and hid behind Elspeth.

Xandie's sleuthing bones were right. The killer had struck again.

"We found him near the graveyard, covered in branches." Braun kneeled next to the late Henry Hedgewater. "I've informed Point Muse and Holly's necromancer bosses at the funeral home. They're coming over in the police cruiser boat later today to pick up both bodies."

Holly worked for Elysian Fields Funeral Home, and her bosses were necromancers and descendants of the ferryman, Charon, the man who ferried the souls of the dead to the underworld...*for a price.* "I'll notify Emmett as well. As the family lawyer, he'll probably have paperwork that needs signing."

Xandie shook her head. "He's locked himself in his room and barricaded the hidden passageway. Lila's delivering food trays to him. He makes her take three steps back before he'll even open the door for her."

Braun stood and dusted his pants off. "Can't say I blame him. Two corpses, a ghost, and a kidnapping would normally make me hightail it to my room if my mom wasn't here to laugh at me."

"Poor baby." Xandie patted Zach's cheek while she winked at him. She sobered. "How did he die?"

"Looks like a tree near the walking path around the graveyard dropped a pile of storm-damaged branches right on top of Hedgewater."

"What a coincidence."

"Not so much. Was the walking a regular pattern for him?"

Xandie nodded. "Every morning. He walked around the island, same time, same path."

Braun pointed to the tree. "There's definitely storm damage, but signs of sabotage as well. Someone rigged the branch to drop when he walked under the tree."

"But how? Anyone could walk this path at any time. The branches might have killed anyone, not just Hedgewater."

Kneeling, Braun lifted thin fishing wire off a branch near the body. "Nope. Our killer booby-trapped the path, probably just before he took his walk. He triggered it and the branches killed him."

"Not an accident?" *Hoping against hope.*

"Not an accident. We need to know where everyone was this morning."

Xandie listed people off with her fingers. "The Harrows, your mom, Marjorie, and I were in the games' room. Emmett in his room. Louisa and David in the kitchen having breakfast. I didn't see Gloria this morning, but Harrison and Herbert were in the games' room with us. Clinton disappeared treasure hunting, so theoretically could have done it, and I didn't see Abigail this morning."

"I saw her in the library." Braun paced. "Anyone in this mausoleum could have snuck out."

"Clinton definitely could have. He has the chops for it. Apparently, he went looking for Henry before we discovered the body, then headed off to the treasure. Plus, if he found the treasure, he'd have to share twenty percent with Henry. With Henry dead, he gets the whole shebang. Sounds like motive to me."

"You don't think he'll find the treasure, do you?"

"Nope. One hundred percent positive Sarah Hedgewater and some loyal servants hid the treasure. Reed will find nothing."

"Let me guess. You know exactly where the treasure is."

"Not quite, but I have a few clues. *In fact...*" Xandie twirled imaginary curls and fluttered her eyelashes. "I know where the next clue is."

"Got something in your eye?"

Note to self, never try flirting again. "I'm heading back inside. I'll let him know."

Braun nodded. "Caleb and Riley are questioning the family. We'll nab Reed when he comes back from hunting his non-existent treasure."

Xandie trudged back to the manor. The Hedgewater family wasn't exactly likeable, but they didn't deserve another death.

"Xandie. Here." Abigail waved Xandie over to the games' room. "Did you find another clue?"

"I have an idea where it is, but I'm more concerned about finding Henry's body."

Abigail covered her mouth in shock. "I'm not getting paid, am I?"

"I thought you were here for the treasure?" Xandie challenged.

"Oh, I am, but I enjoy being paid too," Abigail offered, shamefaced.

Xandie gave the other woman a quick hug. "Let's get this treasure hunt on the road." Stepping into the games' room, she ordered friends and relatives to gather around. "Marjorie, snuff that fire out. Elspeth, when it's out, you need to cool the fireplace down so we can touch it. Everybody else, move back."

The Harrows and their cronies scattered under Xandie's direction.

"Did you find the body?" Holly, wrapped in a blanket, looked miserable.

Kneeling next to her cousin on the couch, Xandie rubbed her leg. "I'm sorry, sweetie. Zach found Henry Hedgewater murdered."

"How?"

"Someone rigged the tree branch to fall. He went out for his morning walk and triggered the fallen branch. Hit him on the head."

Holly shivered. "I thought I'd get used to this death vision thing, but I'm not."

"Kid, that's probably a good thing." Colin poked his head out from underneath the blanket Holly had covered herself with. "Don't let death jade you. You're sweet, toots. Hold on to that. It'll get you more snacks like me."

He waggled his pug eyebrows at Holly.

"That's wrong. Just plain wrong." Sweet wasn't a word Xandie used with the mouthy, flatulence-ridden pug.

Holly smiled faintly. "I'm not wearing a skirt, so he's fine. He's keeping me company, anyway."

"Yeah, skedaddle, Library Girl. I don't share." Colin mock growled and then rolled against Holly's legs.

"All done. This better be good. I don't use my hexes for any old Harrow."

Xandie stepped up to the stone hearth, next to Elspeth. "We have the first direction from Sarah's clue. L.2. I'm positive that means second left. So, wherever her poem leads us, the first direction is to take the second left turn."

"What about the next line we couldn't figure out?" Abigail looked confused.

"'Sit a spell and rest where I found my love, who lit my stone-cold heart.' We found the stone bench. And after Sarah took me on a ghostly adventure last night, I worked out the second bit." Xandie pointed to the fireplace. "Sarah and her lover used to dance in front of the fireplace. Lit my stone-cold heart. Add an *h* to the end of heart and that gives you..." She paused.

"Hearth," Lila and Holly shouted together.

"Exactly." Xandie crouched and bent into the hearth, tracing the side walls with her fingers. *Nothing.* "Come on, Sarah. Help me out a little." A tiny wispy shred of fog drifted to the back of the fireplace. "Thanks," Xandie whispered to her friendly ghost. She ran a hand over the cold stone until she found a raised pattern. "S.H. R.4."

"Sarah Hedgewater. Fourth right turn," Abigail whispered.

Xandie drew back and grimaced at the black soot on her hand. "Correct."

"But we still don't know where to look for Sarah's treasure." Elspeth pouted. "What good are directions if you don't know where to look to begin with?"

"I think I do."

"We never doubted you." Elspeth opened her arms wide. "Never underestimate the Harrow blood line."

Xandie hoped she could live up to her family's lofty expectations. Because she had an awful feeling the killer hadn't finished yet.

SEVENTEEN

"You think you're smart, don't you?" Clinton Reed yanked Xandie away from the dining table where everyone gathered for a buffet lunch.

"Hands off, Reed."

"Or what?"

Elspeth stepped forward and bared her teeth in a predator's grin. "Or I'll break into my box of hex goodies. And who knows what plans the Library has for you?"

Reed moved his hands away from Xandie. "You won't always have your friends around, Librarian."

"I wouldn't bet on that if I were you, Reed." Braun leaned against the dining room door and dangled spelled cuffs from a finger.

"You got nothing on me," Clinton blustered.

"Let's see." Xandie ticked off her fingers. "Kidnapping, assault, theft, and murder. Seems like Braun has a few crimes with your name on them."

"I'll admit to most of those charges but not murder. I didn't touch either Hedgewater. Why should I? Twenty percent is nothing compared to the value of the rest of the treasure."

"You don't even know what's buried. It could be worthless," Xandie scoffed.

"Captain Hedgewater wrote a letter to his banker partner, some guy called Barnes, detailing the contents. Gold, carved chests, spell cauldrons, scrolls. Precious stones and the odd jeweled cross or two. Supposedly totaling millions, according to Henry. Why would I even bother about a measly twenty percent when I have the rest? I don't have to murder anyone, just make a deal."

"Where's the treasure then?" Xandie smirked at the ex-cop. She made an act of peering around him.

Clinton growled at Xandie. "It's gone. All the effort to get past the booby-traps and I found a rotting pirate ship, a few skeletons, and nothing else." Clinton pulled at his hair, only able to make grunting noises as rage gripped his vocal cords.

Gloria moaned. "Typical Hedgewater curse. Finally inherit, and now we get nothing but death and a moldering old house." She slapped her husband on the back of his head. "My mother warned me against you Hedgewaters. She said you were all debt-ridden losers. She wasn't wrong."

Harrison looked wounded. "I thought your mother liked me?"

Sagging back into a chair, Gloria snagged Herbert's glass and slurped a mouthful of the whiskey. "She liked the fact you'd inherit an island. But she'd change her mind if she actually saw this dump."

Clinton recovered his ability to speak. "You still think..." He broke off and bellowed with laughter, slapping at his leg. "The lawyer hasn't told anyone about the will yet?"

Louisa straightened and glared at Reed. "Mr. Emmett is taking his trays in his room."

"That's priceless." Clinton licked his lips. "Sorry to tell you the bad news, Hedgewaters, but neither of the twins inherit now old Henry's kicked the bucket."

Gloria put a hand to her chest. "Me? I inherit? I knew Henry adored me."

Bending over, peals of laughter ripped out of Clinton. Finally, gasping out a breath, he pointed to Louisa. "Old Harry got busy twenty-eight years ago with the house-keeper. She had a kid." He swiveled and then pointed at David, the caretaker. "That kid. He's Hedgewater's heir. He inherits everything. You lot get nothing. Zip, nada." Howling again, he collapsed into a chair at the end of the table.

"You're a damn liar." Herbert stood and kicked his chair away, words slurred.

"I'm afraid Mr. Reed's correct." Emmett, Hedgewater's lawyer, wrung his hands tightly as he stepped into the room. "Mr. Harry invited me to the island two months ago and changed his will in favor of his son."

"Where's the proof he's a Hedgewater?" Harrison pounded the table, spit flying out of his mouth.

Louisa stepped forward. "Look at him and then look at the picture of his father." She pointed to a painting of Harry Hedgewater that rested on the wall above the buffet station. "Same nose, same eyes. If that's not enough proof, read this." Louisa reached into her shirt and drew out a folded piece of paper, which she handed to Xandie.

Opening the document, Xandie turned the paper around and showed it to the room. "Birth certificate for David Riley Mathers. Lists the father as Harry Hedgewater."

Louisa crossed her arms over her chest. "Harry always knew. He sent child support over the years but chose not to have anything to do with his son."

"Until the doctor told him he had limited time left, then he wanted to know me." David hugged his mother. "I wanted nothing to do with him, but Mom insisted, and here we are now."

"It's all confirmed, including a DNA test. David is a Hedgewater." The lawyer shuffled his feet nervously.

Gloria jumped up. "That's it. I'm done. Done with all of you Hedgewaters. I'm moving back in with my mother. Expect divorce papers." She stormed out.

"Gloria, baby. Wait," Harrison wailed and followed her.

Herbert hoisted his glass to his newly discovered cousin. "Hope you find the cursed treasure. Because this place is falling apart." He guzzled the contents of his glass and then leaned back, closing his eyes and snoring lightly.

"Hope you got more of your genes from your mother's side than your father's." Elspeth cackled, and the plates on the table rattled.

Lila sighed. "Do we really need the wicked witch act now, with all the drama we've already had?"

"It's an act?" Marjorie smirked at Elspeth, and they high fived each other.

Abigail narrowed her eyes on David. "Does this mean I might get paid after all?"

David turned to Abigail with a wry smile. "Depends on if we find the treasure in the next few days. Otherwise, I'm selling this place."

"No." Abigail jumped up, shocked. "You can't sell. This is a place of historical significance. Plus, there's treasure hidden somewhere here. It's Sarah's legacy to her family."

David looked troubled. "I feel bad about how the family

treated her, but I'm an ex-soldier. I can't maintain this place without money."

"That's not good enough." Abigail spat the words out and followed Gloria's example by storming away.

"I guess I'm learning Hedgewaters aren't popular." David looked down at his feet.

Poor guy. Xandie couldn't imagine finding out her family were treasure-obsessed douchebags.

Emmett cleared his throat. "If you would come with me, David and Louisa. I have papers for you both to sign." The trio disappeared, leaving the room in silence.

"I might not have found the treasure, but seeing those leeches react is worth its weight in gold."

"Hope your humor sustains you when you're locked up." Braun hauled Reed to his feet and slapped spelled cuffs on him.

Clinton shrugged. "I've got friends in high places. I'll be seeing you treasure hunters sooner rather than later."

Braun led Clinton away.

"As an exit line, that's a great one." Elspeth rubbed her hands together. "Now that our interruptions have left, what's our next treasure hunting step?"

"Fuel up first. Then we figure out the next line. 'Grieve my rest and trace my name to open the way.' Meet back on the front steps in three hours. Gives us enough time to eat and rest. Then we treasure hunt."

And hopefully Sarah still hung around. Because Xandie had a feeling she'd need the ghost's help.

* * *

Elspeth tugged an old-fashioned pith helmet over a short black wig. "I'm ready for anything."

"This isn't a safari adventure. We're treasure hunting." Lila pointed to her grandmother's hat. "And that's a travesty of fashion. But Colin's even worse. I think my eyes are bleeding."

Colin pranced around with a white mosquito net wrapped around his head like a netted halo. "I'm ready for our adventure. Elspeth designed my hat especially for me, kid. I'm a star."

"You're certainly something."

Xandie shot Lila a warning glance. "Where's everybody else?"

"Aggie and Marjorie are monitoring Louisa. She's lying down with a migraine. Probably all the stress of this morning. Winifred's floating around somewhere. The necromancers from Holly's funeral home have picked up the bodies, and Caleb's escorting them back to Point Muse now the boats are running. Emmett's locked up tight in his room. Riley is patrolling around the boathouse, while David is guarding Clinton, and Braun's lurking somewhere outside." Elspeth twitched her helmet again.

"And Holly and Abigail?"

"Right behind you." Holly stood with a downcast Abigail.

"I'm sorry about flipping out earlier. I guess everything got to me."

"You're hanging with the Harrows. Frequent flip out is mandatory." Xandie smiled encouragingly at the girl.

"Enough talking. Where do we go next?"

"Patience, Elspeth." Xandie turned and stared at the graveyard where the monument to Sarah stood like a silent guardian. A wisp of gray wreathed the top of the marker. If Sarah still hovered around, then Xandie could do this.

"The line is... 'Grieve my rest and trace my name to

open the way.'" Xandie pointed to the graveyard. "That's where we're heading."

"What better place to mourn someone's eternal rest than in a graveyard?" Holly smiled proudly at her cousin. "I think my death vibes are rubbing off on you."

"Enough warm fuzzies. Let's hunt." Elspeth took off at a fast clip, with Colin trundling behind, his white mosquito net headwear flapping with him.

The group stood in front of the granite monument to a woman murdered. Sadness for Sarah's fate filled Xandie's throat. Taking a deep breath, she stepped forward as the weak rays of the late afternoon sun shone on the engraved words. "Thanks, Sarah."

Xandie turned and faced her friends and family. "'Grieve my rest and trace my name to open the way.' It's pretty obvious. Sarah's literally telling us what to do." Xandie reached out a hand to Sarah's engraved name on the stone and traced the letters. She reached the last letter in Hedgewater, found a tiny depression, and pushed. Grinding noises echoed through the cemetery, and the monument vibrated. Xandie stepped back quickly as Lila and Holly grabbed her for support.

The paving in front of the monument slowly inched back to reveal carved stone steps covered in cobwebs leading down into the dark. Xandie swept her family a bow. "I give you the way. But we still need to find Sarah's initials and the last path direction."

The Harrows split up and searched around the monument while Abigail stared down into the dark opening.

"Found it." Elspeth pointed to the top of the stone where more writing and Sarah's initials were carved.

"What does that writing above her initials say?"

Xandie's Librarian education didn't stretch to fluency in Latin.

"*Amor aeternus.* Loosely translated, it means love eternal." Elspeth's eyes misted over slightly.

"And the path directions underneath it?" Xandie prodded her unusually sentimental grandmother. Not a normal state for her hard riding, chaos causing grandmother.

"L.1. plus R.2.," Elspeth confirmed.

Xandie consulted her memory. "That makes L.2., R.4., L.1., and R.2. Those are the turns we have to take."

The Harrows returned to Abigail's side, and all the women, plus one pug, stared down into the dark.

"Dibs on not being the spider bait and clearing all the spiderwebs." Holly grabbed a flashlight off Lila as she handed them out.

"You young'uns these days. No staying power. I'll take the lead." Elspeth jacked up her pants and slipped on a headlamp, flicking the light on.

"Wait," Winifred yelled and flapped her hands as she skidded to a stop in front of the group. She bent over, gasping, and held up a finger.

"You okay, Aunt Winifred? Not going to have a heart attack on us?" Xandie bent over next to her aunt and glanced at the woman's fiery red face.

Winifred stood and took a deep breath before exhaling again. "I'm fine. Cardio isn't a Harrow strength. Braun sent me to tell you Clinton escaped. Someone knocked David out while he watched Reed. Braun thinks Clinton might have a partner on the island."

"I bet it's that social climbing Gloria. She dumped Hedgewater. Now she's partnered with the most likely person to find the treasure. Or take the treasure, even if it hurts someone else." Abigail grimaced. "No offense, Xandie. Clinton's more than willing to hurt others for what he wants. Makes his motivation a lot stronger."

Xandie waved her concern away. "We'll keep an eye out for him. At least we know he didn't get here first." She turned to her aunt. "Is Zach okay? Did he get hurt? You can go ahead, and I'll check on him."

"He's fine, sweetie. Annoyed, but fine. Louisa and the rest of the women are doctoring David now and keeping an eye on the other men in case they rush off and do something ridiculously manly and dangerous. I'll head back and tell them where you are, in case of any trouble." Winifred took a deep breath and shuffled off again, this time at a slower pace.

Stubborn and bull-headed, Zach would never admit to knee-jerk reactions, but sometimes Xandie worried he was too much like the Harrow women. Jumping in without thinking his actions through. But if Aggie and the others were looking after him, Xandie could count on them to keep her boyfriend occupied until he needed to spring into action. And she knew how her police chief worked. If her safety was threatened, lickety-split, there'd be a bear shifter guarding the entrance. Xandie made a snap decision. "Rock on, Elspeth. Let's go finish this treasure hunt."

Before the hunt finished them.

"Have I said how grateful I am, Elspeth, for our spider break?" Lila squeaked as a nasty black spider scuttled away from the wicked witch in a safari helmet.

"Ya know, doll face? I'm kind of not loving this tunnel." Spiderwebs hung from Colin's now gray-stained mosquito net.

"Poor puggy wuggy." Elspeth picked up Colin and hoisted him onto a hip. "Don't suppose anyone counted the side passages?"

Dead silence met Elspeth's question. "Seriously?" She spun around, glaring at the girls. "Do I need to do all the work here?"

Abigail scuffed her feet on the dirt passage and raised a hand. "It's the next passage on the left."

Elspeth huffed and paced away to the first turn. "At least one of you knows what a treasure hunt involves."

Xandie hunched her shoulders and followed the rest down the new tunnel. She let her flashlight play over the rough-hewn walls. She had no clue how Sarah and her servants had carved these tunnels without being caught.

Unless there'd already been caves, like underneath the cliff. Solid darkness closed around Xandie before her flashlight blazed again. A scuffle of rock behind her froze Xandie. She held her breath, waiting for another noise, but everything remained quiet.

"You okay, Xandie?" Lila turned back.

Xandie forced a smile. "All good. Thought I heard something behind me, is all."

"You think Clinton's following us?"

"I think we'll definitely see him down here."

"Then we both need to keep up." Lila dragged Xandie to where the others waited.

Elspeth paced as she waited for Xandie. She glared as the duo caught up. "Right, next direction." She speared Xandie in the face with her headlamp. "Chop, chop, Library Girl. We're on the clock."

"Right, fourth tunnel." Xandie turned and whispered to Lila, "What clock are we all on?"

Lila shrugged. "Who knows what level of sanity she's currently swinging with. Go with whatever she says. She's our spider break, remember?"

"Good point."

Abigail dropped back to Xandie and Lila. Holly still stomped single-mindedly behind her grandmother. "Did you see the change in the walls?" Abigail ran her hand carefully over a patch of the wall. "It looks more natural rather than carved. Plus, it's getting colder."

"We must be in the natural cave system under the island. Like under the cliff." Xandie followed Abigail, one hand on the wall. An icy chill spread through her body, itching at the skin. She shivered and wiped dampness on her jeans. "The walls are damp as well. I'd hate to get stuck down here."

"Well, if you don't hurry, I'm leaving you old ladies behind." Elspeth moved Colin across to Holly with a shove of her foot and rolled her sleeves up. "I can feel it. We're getting close. Next direction, Librarian?"

"First left, then second right." Xandie fought the urge to salute her grandmother.

Everyone trooped in a line behind Elspeth. Xandie counted their footsteps. The tunnel felt still around them, the only sound their feet impacting the dirt floor. A double tap behind had her spinning and swinging her light in the tunnel, positive she'd heard steps behind her. Xandie flicked her flashlight from side to side and swore a black shadow darted away into a side tunnel. Clinton had probably followed them. An icy brush on Xandie's shoulder alerted her to Sarah hovering above. "We're almost there. I promise you and Petunia will be free soon." A highflying shadow dropped from the roof, and Xandie fought a bloodcurdling scream.

The shadow alighted on Xandie's shoulder and resolved itself into Petunia, the heart-attack-causing parrot. "Petunia, you nearly caused me to join Sarah in the afterlife."

Petunia shook with her own avian version of a cackle.

Sarah drifted closer, her wispy face more defined as she tried to mouth something to Xandie.

"I'm sorry I don't understand ghost." Xandie tried, but Sarah's face wavered between distinct and foggy which made it near impossible to lip read.

Sarah hovered for a moment and then surged through Xandie.

The walls around Xandie wavered and gave way to the open vista of the island. She stood atop the cliffs, a stiff wind blowing. The island seemed big compared to the contemporary Sarah Island Xandie knew. A shrill scream rang out across the top of the cliff. A no-longer-pregnant Sarah wrestled with an older man with a well-trimmed, gray beard.

Xandie watched as the original Sarah grabbed a rock and slammed it into the side of Hedgewater's head. He bellowed, one hand to his head, and used the other to push his wife off the cliff. Sarah screamed a high-pitched curse of pain upon the family as she soared off the cliff and dropped like a stone. Her husband stumbled back and dropped to his knees before keeling over. The map was a crumpled mess at his feet.

"He had nothing but hate in his heart." A more distinct Sarah, with only a trace of wispy fog, stood next to Xandie. "I pity the poor woman he took as wife eventually, after my death. But I feel more sadness for his descendants. The circle of hate and obsession carried on." Sarah hung her head. "I am not blameless. My curse, uttered in a moment of terror, lasted way too long. I want no more killing in my name. No more obsession and pain visited on the Hedgewater name." The cliff scene wavered, and the tunnel walls solidified around Xandie.

"The Hedgewater bad luck. Your descendants caused the entire family's bad luck, bankruptcy, even death. All Josiah's descendants hated the Hedgewaters."

The ghost drew back from Xandie, and muted shadows ran through the ghostly fog.

Petunia cawed softly to Sarah.

Xandie held out a hand, palms up, making a vow. "You wrote in your journal you didn't want the cycle of hate and obsession to continue. You wanted only peace for the family. I'll make sure your words reach your descendants."

Sarah drifted farther up the tunnel and disappeared.

"You aren't telling anyone anything unless you take me to the treasure. Right now." Clinton appeared next to

Xandie and bent her arm behind her. "I've got friends, little Librarian. I can make those bear shifters pay for any show of defiance from you. The treasure, now."

She trembled, her stomach churning. Petunia had magically disappeared when Sarah had. She couldn't even send the parrot for help.

Clinton shook her arm. "Decide now."

"Fine." Xandie gritted the words out between her teeth. She had no choice. Hopefully, her family had already noticed something was wrong when she didn't appear. They needed to be ready. "Take the first left and then the second right. Let me go, now."

"I don't think so, sweetie. You're my key to unlocking the treasure. Get walking."

Xandie growled but moved forward, counting the tunnels on each side until they hit the first left turn. "It won't help you. Finding the treasure, I mean."

"Finding millions of dollars' worth of treasure sounds good to me."

"The treasure has only ever brought hate and death. Trust me, I've seen it. It's not meant for you."

Clinton shoved Xandie forward as they took the first left turn. "I keep telling people I didn't kill any Hedgewaters. That was someone else on the island."

"Who set you free then?"

"I have no clue. I wasn't even looking at the newest Hedgewater when he got hit. Next thing I know, he's lying at my feet, then someone threw me a key to the spelled cuffs. All I saw was a hooded figure. But whoever freed me did me a favor."

Xandie indicated the last turn, this one on the right. She held her breath as they stepped into a circular cave, with no way out except the way they'd come.

"About time, girl. We had to send Abigail back to get you." Elspeth spun to face Xandie, her face setting firm like stone when she spotted Clinton twisting Xandie's arm behind her back. "Let her go. You don't want to cross me."

"Elspeth? You okay?" Holly looked confused until she followed Elspeth's glare. Her sharp gasp alerted the rest of the family, who stared at Clinton and Xandie.

"Millions of dollars' worth of gold, old woman. I'd cross anyone or anything for much less cash." Clinton waggled Xandie's arm, eliciting a gasp from his prisoner. "Now let's get Operation Make-Clinton-Rich on the road."

Lila stepped forward. "You harm our cousin and Elspeth will hunt you down and destroy you."

"Yeah, my doll face holds a grudge but good. She's mean." Colin's head jerked up and down like a bobble-headed toy dog.

Clinton kicked out his leg and caught Colin on his side, forcing a yelp from the pug.

Elspeth screeched and shot forward, hands with fuchsia-tipped nails extended.

"Back off, or your precious granddaughter's heading for a permanent sleep." Clinton dropped Xandie's arm only to grab her around the neck.

Elspeth lowered her hands and smiled wide, a predator disarming prey. "I'd let my girl go if I were you."

"And why should I?"

"Because the tiny sprite behind you will shoot you otherwise."

Clinton laughed. "You think I'd fall for that, old woman? You're more senile than I thought."

The unmistakable click of a safety switching off filled the room.

Xandie swallowed compulsively as Clinton finally

released her and stepped away, hands in the air. She slowly turned and spotted Abigail standing, legs wide, gun in hand.

"You are a sight for sore eyes, girl. I wondered why it took you so long to find Xandie," Elspeth crowed and twerked her own version of a manic victory dance.

Abigail's gun didn't waver, pointed straight. But not at Clinton... at Xandie.

"Elspeth, you need to rethink the victory dance."

"Why?" Elspeth stopped gyrating and glared at her granddaughter. *"No one interrupts my victory dance..."*

NINETEEN

"Abigail isn't here to help us. She's here to use us to find the treasure."

Stepping forward, Abigail smashed the gun on the back of Reed's head. The ex-cop and kidnapper hit the ground with a meaty thump. She pointed the gun back at Xandie and her family. Her eyes narrowed. "You have no clue what I've had to do. I deserve this. The treasure is mine by right. Not that stupid caretaker's."

"I don't know what's going on." Holly moved closer to Xandie.

The gun's muzzle edged to face Holly. "Move back to your grandmother. All of you, move back."

The Harrows crowded together. All except Colin, who'd disappeared into thin air.

"I don't think Sarah would be happy to see her precious baby Josiah's descendant murdering and hurting people."

"You guessed who I am? Smart Librarian. Sarah was my great, great, whatever. My family name is Barnes, not Berry. Abigail Sarah Barnes."

"You've been killing off the Hedgewaters so you can steal the treasure." Holly nodded, proud of her deduction.

Lila patted her cousin on the arm. "Yes, dear. We worked that out. Try to keep up."

Abigail ignored Xandie's cousins. "My family has pruned the Hedgewater line for a very long time. It's our family duty. Cause pain and destruction to her killer's family and if we get the chance, take the treasure back."

Xandie took a small step forward. She'd hardly paid any attention to the room when she walked in because of Clinton. Now the contents of the small cavern registered...*or the lack of contents*. The small space was empty except for a large statue carved into the rock of the wall. The Greek goddess, Aphrodite. Xandie smiled. The last few lines of Sarah's poem were obvious now. She focused back on Abigail. "She'd have hated this killing. Sarah bitterly regretted playing into Hedgewater's treasure obsession. Aside from leaving her baby, that curse she uttered as she died is one of her biggest regrets."

"Enough!" Abigail screamed. "Sarah wanted us to hurt the Hedgewaters. Josiah's father wrote everything down in his own journal. The Barnes family throughout the years have always carried out his wishes."

Xandie took out Sarah's journal and held it up. "Yeah, I've got a journal too. Sarah's journal."

"No more talk." Abigail took two steps forward, the gun now pointing straight at Xandie's face.

A gray wisp floated behind Abigail. *Sarah.* Xandie nodded. "Fine. You want the treasure, take it." She swept her arms around the empty room.

"Where is it?" Abigail screeched.

Elspeth cleared her throat. "We only found the statue. We were waiting for Xandie to come and work it out for us."

Calming herself, Abigail smiled sweetly and pointed the gun at Elspeth. "Find my treasure or your grandmother dies first."

Xandie held a hand up and turned to the statue. "It's a statue of the Greek goddess of love, Aphrodite."

"I don't care what the dumb thing is. Find my treasure."

"You should care. Sarah did." Xandie grazed a fingertip across the goddess's face. "The last few lines of Sarah's clue. 'Unlock the path to seek the fortune.' We've already done that. 'Well hidden, with love's touch.'" Xandie let her hand drift down to the statue's heart. "You love someone with all your heart, all it needs is love's touch." Xandie pressed a hand over the statue's heart.

A grating whir echoed in the cave. The statue slid to the side in fits and jerks until the stone goddess of love revealed a small room...and three barrels, four wooden chests, a spell cauldron, and piles of gold, silver, and precious stones.

"Finally." Abigail breathed the word into the quiet moment, everyone else silent as they took in the sight of the treasure.

A little dark shadow on four legs darted into the treasure room and behind a chest.

Abigail took a stumbling step toward the cache of gold.

"I showed you the treasure. Now let us go." Xandie knew there was a snowball's chance in the underworld that the treasure-obsessed Abigail would release them. But she had to try.

Tearing her attention from the piles of gold, Abigail laughed hysterically at Xandie's words. "Are you that naïve? I've killed, murdered those filthy Hedgewaters, and you can identify me. I'm afraid you're going to have a tragic accident while hunting the cursed treasure. Cave-ins happen regularly here, I'm sure."

Holly sobbed quietly while Elspeth and Lila comforted her.

Another flicker of wispy gray appeared behind Abigail, solidifying until the ghostly, luminescent features of Sarah appeared.

Xandie pointed to the ghost. "I think your ancestor, Sarah, has something to say about that."

Abigail spun and confronted Sarah. A glowing Petunia squawked overhead, alighting on Abigail's shoulder. Sarah surged into her descendant. Abigail's back arched, and her mouth opened in a silent scream as the gun dropped from her paralyzed hands to the ground.

Darting in, Xandie snatched the gun and waved her family over. "You guys need to get out of here and grab Braun. He can secure Clinton and Abigail."

Lila's eyes rounded as the outside of Abigail began to glow with an unearthly blue light. "What is that?"

"Sarah. Showing Abigail the error of her ways. Sarah never wanted her descendants to obsess over the treasure like the Hedgewaters. Unfortunately, it didn't work out that way."

Holly stiffened and turned faintly silvered eyes on Xandie. "I think we need to get out of here." As she spoke, a low rumbling noise echoed through the tunnels. The room shook, and the women held on tightly to each other.

Abigail stopped screaming and slumped to the ground, mumbling to herself, "A ghost. Saw a ghost. Sarah. Needs it all to end." She repeated the phrase over and over.

Sarah and Petunia shimmered next to Xandie. The bird was no longer corporeal but just as mouthy. "Pieces of eight, ya old bats." Petunia dropped an old Spanish coin into Xandie's hand.

"Pieces of eight, Petunia." Xandie stared at Abigail. "I'll

make sure Josiah's family never seek vengeance on the Hedgewater family in your name again."

Sarah's ghostly hand trailed over the journal that had fallen to Xandie's feet in the rush to get to the gun.

"I know. I'll give it to them." Xandie smiled through tears at Sarah. "You and Petunia rest. Meet your son."

Sarah lifted a hand in goodbye, and with a last squawk, Petunia dive-bombed the Harrow women with a final Elspeth-like cackle before returning to Sarah. They slowly disappeared.

Another rumble shook the room, and Colin scooted out of the treasure stash, jingling as he ran.

Xandie handed the gun and journal to Lila and picked up the panting pug.

Yelling reached the women's ears as Braun, Riley, and David rushed into the cave.

Braun grabbed Xandie in a tight hug. "You're always trouble, Meyers."

One arm hoisting Colin onto her hip, Xandie snuggled into Zach's warm embrace. "I keep telling you. It's the Harrow in my blood. You can blame Elspeth."

The rumbling grew louder, and Braun reluctantly disengaged from Xandie. "Caleb, grab Reed. David, can you get Abigail out? The rest of you, skedaddle. This whole place is becoming unstable."

As one, the group raced out of the cavern, everyone following Elspeth as she led the way out of the tunnels.

Braun whispered to Xandie as they followed, "Do I want to know where she got the pith helmet?"

"Probably not." Elspeth always dressed for the occasion *and* the odd cave fall. Xandie stifled a faintly hysterical snicker as they emerged into the graveyard. "Everyone, hold on," Xandie yelled as even the island shook, followed by a loud boom. Dust flew from the passageway under the stone monument.

"Well, there goes my inheritance." David looked resigned but not overly upset.

"Not entirely." Xandie held Colin up in the air and gave him a little shake. The pug clinked and clanked like a jingle bell recital. Xandie placed him on the ground and unwound the stained mosquito net from around his neck. Gold and silver coins, along with colorful, precious stones, tumbled onto the grass. Xandie eyed the plug sternly. "Colin?"

Colin wrinkled his pug nose. "It's my finder's fee. That pirate booty would buy a lot of snacks." His eyes suddenly gleamed. "Or fresh tuna."

As one, the Harrow women shuddered and shouted, "No."

Xandie scooped up the pirate treasure in the mosquito net and dumped it into David's arms. "That should get you floated. Hire some experts and get the treasure excavated safely."

David shook his head, dazed. "Thank you. That's all I can say. Thank you."

"It was time. Sarah and Petunia needed to rest. They've been waiting a very long time to join their family." Xandie smiled and lifted her head to the late afternoon sun, feeling the warmth of a good deed done well.

Sometimes. Just sometimes. Things ended the way they were supposed to. *Even for a Harrow...*

TWENTY

"Thank you so much for helping us." Louisa gave Xandie a tight hug and then stepped back to stand with her son.

The police cruiser boat stood moored next to the dock. Caleb and Riley had already escorted Reed and a still dazed Abigail on board in spelled cuffs. Aggie and Marjorie argued while they climbed into the cruiser.

"Harrows aren't known for helping, more like meddling," Lila muttered.

"Meddling, helping. Same thing to me." Elspeth eyed her granddaughter. "Stand straight, no slouching. You'll never land a husband like that."

Snickering, Holly waggled her eyebrows. "It's more like catch and release for the Harrows."

Elspeth threatened Holly with an outstretched hand. "Pull my finger. I dare you." Blue electricity arced between her fingers.

Winifred rolled her eyes and grabbed her daughter and mother, shoving them toward the police cruiser.

Louisa laughed, and the sun glittered off the auburn strands of her hair.

Warmth spread through Xandie as the last piece finally slotted into place. "Did you know you're related to Sarah?"

"I wondered when you'd figure it out. But yes, I've always known. My branch of the family broke away. Wanted no part of the search and destroy Barnes family mission. Then I met Harry. He seemed much nicer back then, even dashing. I didn't care he was a Hedgewater."

"And then along came David."

Louisa linked an arm with her son. "As far as I'm concerned, *he* was my treasure. But after the Army, David needed something else in his life. I spoke to Harry, and we came here. Surprisingly enough, they hit it off. At least enough for Harry to change his will."

A beam of light centered on Louisa and David. Her auburn hair and the same hazel eyes as the Sarah in the portrait. The resemblance was so obvious now. David had Hedgewater eyes but Sarah's stubborn chin. Sarah and Captain Hedgewater had come full circle. One of their descendants, now joining both bloodlines. Together in peace like Sarah wanted. Xandie mentally blew Sarah and Petunia a goodbye kiss.

Braun hugged Xandie to his side. "All's well that ends well. At least, as good as it gets for the Harrows anyway. Now a long vacation from body finding would be perfect."

Famous last words...

The end.

Want More?

You can sign up for my mailing list. It's for new releases and no spam. Be the first to grab specials, new releases, and freebies.

Sign up now

https://www.kellyethan.com/newsletter

LEAVE A REVIEW

Did you like this book?

Please leave a review for it on Amazon!

The Vengeful Villain and the Cursed Treasure

ABOUT THE AUTHOR

I want to thank everyone who spent the time to read my novel.

My world is small town magic, mystery and mayhem, with plenty of snarky laughs along the way.

With an overactive imagination and a love of all things that go bump in the night, it was natural to write cozy paranormal mysteries, but I also love paranormal romance. No matter the genre, I love sarcastic heroines who like to save the day and solve the puzzle.

With a busy and chaotic household, writing is my outlet for madness. I live in Australia and when not writing, I can be found plotting my next fictional murder or chasing after the family's ferocious hellhound.

Visit me today at my website or say hello on social media.

Website:
https://www.kellyethan.com

facebook.com/KellyEthanWriter

instagram.com/kellyethanauthor

tiktok.com/@authorkellyethan

COZY PARANORMAL MYSTERY:

Point Muse Cozy Paranormal Mystery Series

The Wicked Witch and the Christmas Chaos
The Wicked Witch and the Stolen Snow Globe
The Conniving Carver and the Jeering Jack-O-Lantern
The Wicked Witch and the Ultimate Smackdown
The Wicked Witch and the Abominable Snowman
The Wicked Witch and the Killer Grinch

#0 The Pernicious Pixie and the Choked Word
#1 The Killer Knight and the Murderous Chairleg
#2 The Dastardly Dragon Killer and the Poisoned Breath
#3 The Murderous Monster and the Stony Gaze
#4 The Cursed Crow and the Deadly Hex
#5 The Slanderous Siren and the Grievous Gift
#6 The Vengeful Villain and the Cursed Treasure
#7 The Fiendish Foe and the Deadly Jewels
#8 The Nefarious Nemesis and the Wedding Jinx

ALSO BY KELLY ETHAN

Point Muse Cozy Paranormal Mystery Boxed Set: Books 1-3

Point Muse Cozy Paranormal Mystery Boxed Set: Books 4-6

Point Muse Cozy paranormal Mystery Boxed Set: Books 1-8

LILA HARROW: Point Muse Cozy Paranormal Mystery

Cookies, Curses and Christmas Corpses.
#1 Cupcakes, Corpses and Chaos
#2 Pies, Potions and Peril
#3 Sin, Sugar and Shadows
LILA HARROW Point Muse Boxed Set: Books 1-3

HOLLY HARROW: Point Muse Cozy Paranormal Mystery

Banshee, Vikings and Voodoo
#1 Banshee, Death and Disarray
#2 Banshee, Moonshine and Madness
#3 Banshee, Sea Monster and Sabotage
HOLLY HARROW Point Muse Boxed Set: Books 1-3

The Ghost Vein Mine Cozy Paranormal Mysteries

#1 Ghosts and Gold Dust
#2 Curses and Cold Cases

Non Fiction

Heart and Craft.